EXTINCTION: UNDEAD APOCALYPSE

THEM POST-APOCALYPTIC SERIES BOOK FIVE

M.D. MASSEY

MODERN DIGITAL PUBLISHING

This story is focused on Scratch Sullivan. I thought it was only proper to make this novel about his trials and travails exclusively since this is more or less his final send-off.

So, if you're expecting to spend a lot of time with the supporting characters from the previous novels, you may be disappointed. Certainly, Gabby, Bobby, the Doc, and yes, even Colin are very much present throughout most of the book. However, they are relegated to supporting roles, more so than in any previous volume in this series.

I wanted this to be Scratch's story, and so it is. I hope you enjoy it.

~M.D. Massey

DREAMERS

Soldiers are citizens of death's grey land,
Drawing no dividend from time's to-morrows.
In the great hour of destiny they stand,
Each with his feuds, and jealousies, and
    sorrows.
Soldiers are sworn to action; they must win
Some flaming, fatal climax with their lives.
Soldiers are dreamers; when the guns begin
They think of firelit homes, clean beds
    and wives.

I see them in foul dug-outs, gnawed by rats,
And in the ruined trenches, lashed with rain,
Dreaming of things they did with balls and bats,
And mocked by hopeless longing to regain
Bank-holidays, and picture shows, and spats,
And going to the office in the train.

~Siegfried Sassoon

GUNS

We were pinned down in a row house that we'd picked at random from a sea of row houses, in some nameless town roughly a third of the way between Austin and the Facility. We'd chosen to bed down here because the house was mostly intact, nondescript, and close to a safe house that I'd been looking for the day before.

We'd spent an hour looking for that safe house. I could have sworn it was in this neighborhood—right on this street, in fact. But apparently, my memory was just one item on a long list of things that weren't working right since our run-in with the Corridor Pack and Piotr, the genocidal vampire from hell. I'd taken a hell of a blow during my very brief fight with him, and even days after the concussion, my brain still wasn't functioning at optimal capacity. My thoughts were fuzzy, and according to Bobby and Gabby, I'd just zone out at odd times—sort of like I was having a petit mal seizure.

I figured that the serum was still in a pissing contest with the deader venom inside my body, and that must've been slowing down my body's ability to heal. Normally, someone who was juiced on the Doc's super-serum would have bounced back from a head injury in a day or two. But me? My body had been fighting off the effects of a deader bite since I'd first gone under the Doc's needle. And despite the best that millions of dollars of Uncle Sam's research money and years of experimentation could come up with, the Doc still couldn't create a way to reverse the effects of getting bitten by a shambler.

Sure, the Doc's serum could make you move faster, jump higher, and hear and smell better than a normal human being. But it couldn't make you immune to deader bites. The way the Doc explained it, you'd have to be a full-on 'thrope to be immune; a little gene therapy and borrowing a few of their finer traits just wasn't good enough. The Doc swore that she thought the serum would eventually fight off the deader vyrus running through my body. I wondered how many other poor Army schmucks had died testing that hypothesis over the years. Not to mention how many of those poor souls had died under the effects of the Doc's needle.

Didn't matter, anyway. Kara was a vampire now, and chances were good that she was never coming back to me—vamps and hunters didn't mix. And what good would it do to have my health, knowing that she was out there suffering? I hated myself for letting her down, just as much as I hated all the self-loathing I'd been doing. I'd gotten so low that I was hating the part of me that hated myself. Shit, how screwed up was that?

A bullet pinged off a cast-iron skillet next to me and brought me out of my thoughts. I looked up and saw Gabby returning fire from behind an overturned refrigerator, and Bobby was in my face yelling something I couldn't understand. But I heard the sounds of gunfire, both from Gabby's Glock and outside the windows. Broken glass flew, drywall dust floated in the air, and over it all there was a dull roar inside my head, like the sound of a tsunami making landfall, just before it destroyed everything in its path. Bobby's voice sounded like it was coming from a million miles away. I tuned out the roar and focused on his voice.

"Scratch! Scratch, buddy, come back to me—I need you with us or we're all going to die here, and that's not on my five-year plan. Well, maybe I won't die per se—but you and Gabby sure will."

I stared at him like a calf at a new gate. Gabby was swapping out mags, and she had a piece of window casing sticking out of her left hand. The wood splinter was white where it had been painted to contrast the light tan paint on the walls, and yellow where the pine had splintered away from the window. She was covered in drywall dust and sweat, and drops of blood swelled around her wound and caught the light from outside as it flooded in through the broken window next to her. As I gazed absently at the wound on her hand, she spared me a look that was two parts incredulity and one part disgust.

Apparently, I'd been lost inside the wasteland of my mind for a while. The last thing I remembered was gunshots shattering the glass in the kitchen window. Prior to that, this place had been more or less intact.

Shit.

I glanced back to Bobby and looked him in the eye for a split second, then brushed the broken glass and drywall dust off me.

"Stop yelling," I said quietly. I looked around and grabbed an AK-47 that I'd liberated from a punter a few days before, pulling back and releasing the charging handle. Once I was sure the safety was off, I stood up. Bullets were still flying all around me, but I really didn't care all that much. I calmly sauntered out the side door of the house, shouldering the rifle as I walked at a leisurely pace around the front of the building.

As I rounded the corner, I dropped two punters with precise, almost casual shots to the head and torso. *Pop. Pop-pop.* One fell instantly to a head shot. The other slumped slowly over the hood of the car he was using for cover, then slid down the side, leaving a large bloody smear on the dull white paint of the hood.

It took a moment for the other three punters to recognize me as a threat, and that was the only reason I didn't get shot. Well, that and luck. They eventually turned their guns on me, but by the time they'd reacted I was already rolling over the attackers, just like the tidal wave roaring in my head.

A round grazed my shoulder and another whizzed past my face, so close I swear I could feel the heat as it zipped by. I hit a punter in the neck with a single, carefully-aimed shot, and blood spurted from the wound onto his buddy next to him. Or at least, I assumed they were buddies, since they were accomplices in an attempt on our lives. Maybe they hated each other; it didn't matter. I put two rounds in the other guy's chest while he was still wiping blood out of his eyes.

I shot the last one in the back as he was running away from me.

I stopped in the middle of the street, slowly swiveling my head for more threats. There were none. So, I dropped my rifle and pulled a pack of cigarettes out of my shirt pocket. Nasty habit—one that I'd taken up again since Austin had happened.

I pulled the filter off a cigarette and lit up as I wondered absently whether the Doc's serum could halt the growth of lung cancer. A few moments later, Bobby came running out of the house screaming at me, his face a mask of contempt and disbelief.

The young 'thrope lifted me effortlessly by my lapels, his were-wolf strength on full display as he handled me like a man would a child. My back slammed up against a broken-down Chevy and the driver's window shattered with the violence of the impact. Bobby's curled up fists and elbows pressed into my ribcage, and he growled in my face. I checked my cigarette to make sure the cherry hadn't fallen off, and took another drag.

Bobby frowned, sighed, and let me go. I rolled my shoulders out and checked them for injuries; I'd have bruises for sure, and wake up stiff and sore tomorrow. Otherwise, no broken bones. Guess he was just trying to see how I'd react.

He stepped back and rubbed a hand across his face. "Scratch, what the hell was that?"

I looked away, rolling the cigarette between my fingers. Funny how those cancer sticks could be so comforting and calming. And addicting. It had taken me forever to shake the habit when I'd come back from Afghanistan; if I got hooked now, I'd be screwed. Pre-war cigarettes were damned hard to come by, and folks who grew tobacco sold it at a premium. I'd lucked out by finding a half-carton in one of the houses we'd flopped in that first night out of Austin. Chances were good I wouldn't be so lucky in days to come.

I addressed Bobby's question, staring off into space. "You said you thought we were going to die. From the way Gabby was shooting, I figured it was likely. So, I stopped that from happening."

He ran his fingers through his sandy, sunkissed hair. "I get that, Scratch—and don't get me wrong, I'm pleased as punch that you decided to chip in and help. But that stunt you just pulled almost got you killed."

"I'm still standing. So are you and Gabby." I waved my cigarette at the dead bodies around us. "They aren't. Problem solved."

Bobby sighed again through his nostrils. "You know, I expected you to be all broken up over what happened in Austin with Kara. Heck, I even expected you to fall apart a little. But what I didn't expect was for you to full-on puss out with all this nihilist bullshit."

He glared at me from under his eyebrows, sea-blue eyes lit up by the sunlight reflected on the chrome trim of the Chevy. "You're a grown man, and you've lived this shit just as long as we have. You know things like this aren't just a possibility—they're a probability, a fact of life for the world we live in. Yet you have the nerve to act like this sort of thing shouldn't happen to you or the people you care about."

I spat a fleck of tobacco to the side and shrugged. "It was your fault those punters found us in the first place. If you hadn't gotten greedy and stolen an entire roasted boar from them, this never would have happened."

He threw his hands up in the air and rolled his eyes. "Oh, that's great—just brilliant. Shift the blame to me because I was trying to look out for us." He poked me in the chest and narrowed his eyes. "If you didn't have your head up your ass, I might have been able to split off and do some actual hunting. But no, I don't have time for that, because I have to be looking out for both you and Gabby. So, I had to make do. Sue me."

I stifled a yawn. "You could have done it in wolf form. No way they'd track a 'thrope to get back their meal. That would've kept them off our backs and filled our bellies. But I guess I'm the only one who thinks about stuff like that." At this point, I was just pouring salt on an open wound, but I'd had enough of his attitude. I liked Bobby a lot, but this self-righteous crap had its limits.

He placed his hands on his hips and looked up at the sky for a moment. Then his gaze locked on mine. "You know what pisses me off the most about you running around in this idiotic self-hating fugue state? The fact that she has to suffer for it."

He pointed off at the house, where I could see Gabby puttering around the place, gathering our gear—and trying to act like she most definitely wasn't listening in on our conversation. Bobby squatted and picked up my rifle, then stood and shoved it into my chest.

"Just consider that you're not the only one who's hurting right now. Gabby's been through a lot over the past several weeks, and most of it is because she got caught up in your wake."

I grabbed the rifle with one hand and took a last, long drag off the cigarette with the other. Bobby leaned forward until our faces were within kissing distance. He hissed his last words with so much venom I could almost feel the syllables stripping the skin from my face.

"Get your shit together before you get her killed, or worse. Because if anything ever happens to her and I think you're responsible for it, it won't matter whether I see you as my alpha or not... I'll make sure you pay for it."

I let him stalk off without giving a response, mostly because he was right about me being an asshole. I was letting my emotions affect everyone else around me. And since it was just him and Gabby at the moment, they'd been taking the full brunt of my self-pity and picking up the slack during my mental and emotional absence.

Damn it. I'd never fathered a child, but I was doing the absentee father thing like a pro. I needed to lock this shit down before I really did get us killed. I mulled it over as Gabby walked out of the house.

She strolled over and dropped my ruck at my feet. "We gotta go—deaders heard the gunfight. More'll be here soon." She pointed up and down the street at two small crowds of groaning shamblers that were moving toward our position.

I stared at the ground for a moment, trying hard to show some concern on my face before I made eye contact with her. She was looking at me with her head cocked at a slight angle, and her eyes were serious, but not unkind. It would be clear to anyone who looked into those baby browns that this kid was wise and mature well beyond her years. I thought about how hard it must be to be a tween on the outside, sixteen on the inside, and have a soul that was closing in on fifty.

I took a deep breath and let it out. "Sorry I'm letting you down, kid."

She shrugged. "It's allowed. You're only human, you know."

I chuckled. "Not anymore. And it remains to be seen whether I'll keep what little humanity I have left." I pulled up my sleeve, where the deader virus appeared to be making a resurgence. Black veins and lines spread from the scar to my elbow and down into my hand. "You never know, I might just wake up a biter one day."

She cocked a fist and tapped me on the jaw with it. "You're too ugly and stupid to be a deader, *pendejo*. I know you're hurting, but you need to suck it up so we can get back to the Facility alive. You can take all the time you need to mourn once we get there."

I nodded. "Gabby, I don't think I've ever told you, but I'm proud of you. Did you know that?"

"I know," she replied. "It's why I keep sticking around. Well, that and my father issues—or, at least, that's what Bobby keeps saying."

I harrumphed at that. "Don't sweat it, kid. We all have them and have to deal with them at some point."

She smirked. "I'm supposed to watch some *Oprah* reruns with him when we get back. He says it'll help me get in touch with my inner goddess or something. Sounds like *cagada* to me, but what do I know?" The moans were getting louder, and I could hear the shuffling footsteps of the dead to either side of us. Gabby cracked her neck and nudged me with an elbow. "Time to go, *viejo*, unless you want to be on the menu."

I shouldered my pack and pointed with my chin in a southernly direction. "Lead the way."

Bobby caught up to us a few blocks down the road, and we walked in silence for much of the day. I regretted not taking the time to strip the punters for ammo and gear, but that was just one more example of how my self-pity was hurting the group. I thought about it as the day wore on and we stewed in our own reticence. That was just as well, since we ran across more punters later in the day.

We were skirting San Marcos when they burst across the road not a hundred yards in front of us, running like a pack of scalded dogs. We found concealment on the side of the road and took up defensive positions to see what was chasing them. They were definitely punters and not carvaneers, no doubt about it. No one but punters dressed like *Road Warrior* rejects out here in the Badlands, plus I picked up a stench coming off them from a hundred yards away. There were cannibals among them; the smell was unmistakable. It was in their clothes, and they were sweating it out of their pores. We were lucky the last group we'd come across hadn't been eating long pig, but real pig instead. Otherwise, we might have gone hungry.

Suddenly the thought of Bobby stealing an entire pig right off the spit made me chuckle, and that earned me a weird look from Gabby. She duckwalked over to me and whispered just loud enough for the three of us to hear.

"What do you think has them running like that?"

I chewed my lip and stared as the last one darted across the road. "No idea, but it has to be bad." I turned to Bobby. "Follow them and snag a straggler. Gabby and I will set up in that greenhouse we saw a few miles back and meet you there."

Bobby arched an eyebrow, then shrugged and slipped away soundlessly. Gabby looked at me, and I tilted my head toward the direction we'd come from. I took off at a trot, and she followed in silence.

Half an hour later, we were questioning the punter Bobby had snatched. He was a youngish guy—early twenties, rangy and dangerous-looking in a rat-faced sort of way. He was wearing a long black trench coat and Doc Martens, along with a filthy pair of jeans and two sliced up concert t-shirts layered one over the other. A spiked dog collar topped off the whole "Sid Vicious in the apocalypse" look. Based on the condition of the boots and coat compared to his other clothes, I figured he'd salvaged or stolen them recently; they were almost serviceable.

We tied him to a rickety aluminum lawn chair with a length of garden hose, inside a greenhouse that had probably fed a lot of people before the War. Holes in the roof provided moisture for the plants inside, which were now overgrown and neglected. Wildlife had eaten most of the bounty, but Gabby had found a few overripe tomatoes that had escaped their notice. She was sitting atop a table off to the side, eating them with the juice running down her chin and fingers.

Our guest was staring at her, which I suppose he preferred over staring at me or Bobby. Bobby was slowly shredding the table he was sitting on with his nails, which at the moment were longer and sharper than they had a right to be. *Skritch. Skritch. Skritch.* In the short time since he'd arrived with the punter, Bobby had generated quite a pile of splinters and wood shavings.

I had to admit, for a goofy surfer kid, he sure knew how to put the fear in someone.

I walked around behind the guy and placed my hands on his shoulders. He stank of sweat, body odor, and cooked human flesh. I wasn't going to let him live, but he didn't know that.

Although, if he had half a brain he'd assume the same. I leaned over his shoulder and whispered in his ear.

"What were you running from?"

He broke like a toppled gum ball machine, with words spilling all over the place. "Oh, is that all you want to know? Man, I thought you were going to eat me or something. Shit. You nearly had me pissing my pants over here."

He craned his neck to look back at me, but I was gone, already stalking around his other side. Before he turned his head back to see where I'd disappeared to, I slammed my hands down over his wrists on the arms of the lawn chair. I leaned in close, close enough to smell his rank breath. He shied away from the look in my eyes, and despite the chill in the air, a bead of sweat drew a lazy line down his forehead.

"Talk," I growled.

"Okay, no problem. I'll tell you why we're running, and this is no bullshit." He took a deep breath and closed his eyes, then opened them and let it out. "It's them demon dogs, man."

Gabby chortled and nearly spit out a mouthful of tomato. Bobby stopped scratching the table and stared at the guy. Wild dogs and coywolves could be an issue to lone travelers, but they tended to shy away from large groups and settlements. I picked up my left foot and placed it ever so gently right on top of the punter's nut sack, and leaned in a little. He groaned and tried to scoot back in the seat to relieve the pressure.

"I'm serious, man! No bullshit—these mean-ass demon dogs have been attacking us. They look kind of like regular dogs, like German Shepherds or Rottweilers or some crap like that. 'Cept they're *not* dogs—at least, not like any I've seen."

Gabby frowned and spoke up from where she sat. "What the hell are you going on about?"

The punter blinked and shook his head. "I knew you wouldn't believe me."

He looked down at my boot on his crotch. I relieved the pressure and nodded. "Go on."

He let out a sigh of relief, and closed his eyes as he grimaced before relaxing somewhat. "It started about a week ago. People were going missing at night. First one, then two, then more. We could never see what was doing it, and we started locking ourselves in at night. Then, they came for us during the day.

"I'm telling you, these freaking things are pure evil. They're mean as hell, they never bark, and their eyes glow like you're shining a light at them, even in the daytime."

Bobby scratched his head and took a deep breath. "They don't sound like werewolves, that's for sure. Sounds more like Cujo to me."

The guy shook his head vigorously. "No, these ain't no 'thropes—but they're smart. They worked together to separate a few of our people from the group. Then, they tore them to shreds. But they never eat anything they kill; they just leave it there to rot. So, after half of us got killed by 'em, we all grabbed our shit and split. They've been following us and picking the rest of us off ever since."

Of course, a part of me remained skeptical about his story. But if this punter was telling the truth, there might be a new threat in the area. I racked my brain and tried to recall whether I'd ever heard of this happening before. Something niggled the back of my mind, but I just couldn't make the connection. I pulled up a stool in front of him, and leaned forward on my elbows.

"Tell me more about these dogs. In fact, tell me everything you know. Leave nothing out."

I INTERROGATED the guy for the better part of an hour, trying to see if he'd change his story or alter the timeline in any way under pressure or fatigue. But he stuck to the same story, same facts, and same descriptions of the mysterious dog attacks that had been plaguing their punter group for days.

When I was through with him, I walked to the other side of the greenhouse and beckoned Bobby and Gabby to follow.

"So, what do you two think about his story?"

Bobby shrugged. "As far as I can tell, he's not lying. I'd say he believes what he's telling us, every single word."

I nodded. "Gabby, what's your opinion?"

Gabby rubbed her chin with her thumb and forefinger, staring off into space. "I don't know, Scratch. I agree that he's telling the truth. But as far as what these things are, it's anybody's guess." She inhaled quickly and let her breath out through pursed lips. "But one thing's for sure—those punters were running from something. I suppose anything is possible."

I scratched my head. "Have either of you ever heard of anything like this before?"

Bobby nodded enthusiastically. "Oh yeah. Well, I mean, not

like this—but I've seen some strange stuff that's at least as weird as what we just heard."

Gabby frowned and looked at Bobby with suspicion. "Like what?"

He crossed his arms and tilted his head at her. "Would you be surprised to know that I've met a chupacabra?"

Gabby rolled her eyes and laughed. "Oh boy, here we go with this story again." She must have seen the confusion on my face, because she turned to me and grinned. "Oh, you haven't heard about this yet? Bobby claims to have spent several days traveling with a chupacabra. He claims the thing latched on to him like a groupie and wouldn't leave him alone."

She circled a finger in the air next to her head and made a dopey expression. "I think maybe he ate some *peyote* by accident, and dreamed the whole thing."

Bobby stuck his palm out in front of her face. "Fine, believe what you want. But when those little goat-suckers show up to drink your blood from between your toes, don't come crying to me."

I momentarily tried to make sense of what he'd just said, then realized making sense out of any of the crazy stuff Bobby said was an exercise in futility. I shook my head and sighed. "Toe-sucking chupacabras? I don't even want to know."

Gabby smirked again. "Anyway, getting back to what we were talking about a minute ago. I know someone who was a hunter before the War, kind of like Rabbi Manny but not as weird. He doesn't live too far from here; maybe we could take a detour and ask him if he's ever heard of something like these *perros diablos?*"

I rubbed my neck. "Well, I suppose it couldn't hurt. How far?"

Gabby shrugged. "Fifteen miles, maybe. It's north and just a little past Canyon Lake. Maybe we could stop in and see Bernie and Margaret while we're at it?"

Truth be told, I really just wanted to get back to a warm bunk and sleep for a couple of days straight. Plus, I was eager to see how the Colin's Wild Boys had fared in ferrying the settlers we rescued back to the Facility. But considering what an asshole I'd been lately, I couldn't see any reason to say no to the side trip.

"Alright, we'll head over to see your friend, and we can stop by Canyon Lake on the way."

Bobby rubbed his hands together with glee. "Yes! Margie sure can cook a mean fish soup. I get dibs on fish heads!"

Gabby chose to ignore Bobby's gonzo outburst and instead gestured at the punter sitting across the greenhouse from us. He was eyeing us warily, and looked to be fairly worried about his immediate future.

"What should we do with him?" she asked me with concern in her voice.

I thought about it for a moment, and realized I was too tired to want to kill the kid—cannibal or not. "Cut him loose. He's not worth the trouble to kill, and I don't want to draw any vamps on our trail by leaving blood behind."

Her shoulders dropped slightly at my response, and Bobby let out a small sigh of relief. I hadn't noticed how tense they were until they registered my response. It made me wonder just how much of a flake I'd been, to put these two on edge over the last few days.

Gabby was about to release our prisoner when I grabbed her shoulder to stop her. "You know what? I'll do it, while you and Bobby plan a route to your friend's place. Besides, the less I hear Mr. Motormouth jabber about eating fish heads, the better."

Bobby grinned ear to ear. "You don't know what you're

missing out on, Scratch. I'm telling you, sucking the eyeballs out is the best part."

"Yeah, I'll pass. I ate enough weird stuff when I was in the military. I'll tell Margie to give you my share."

Bobby slapped me on the back. "You're a real pal, Scratch."

I nodded slowly. "Don't mention it."

We hiked west and arrived at the Canyon Lake settlement around noon. Other than a few shamblers who tagged along, the trip itself was uneventful. Margie gave us all hugs as we walked up to the docks, and Bernie gave me a firm handshake and an appraising look after I escaped Margie's grasp.

"You look like hell."

I nodded. "I feel like hell, Bernie."

"Well, the world's not kind, but I have some scotch that'll fix that right up." He headed to the main building and motioned for me to tag along. I followed after him, leaving Bobby and Gabby to his wife's kind ministrations.

Once inside, we headed up to the deck to sip whiskey while we made small talk. Eventually, Bernie broke the ice.

"So, you going to tell me what tore you up and spat you out since we seen you last?"

I looked out the window and cleared my throat. "You remember where we were headed, right? To save my girl Kara and the rest of the settlers?"

He sipped his whiskey. "I do. And, as I recall, I said you were headed into a shit storm. I take it things didn't go so well?"

I shrugged. "We got most of the settlers back, at least the women and children. There's some of your people in the group we rescued, Bernie. Sorry that I forgot to ask names before they left for the Facility."

He smiled. "That is good news. Marge will be glad to hear it. Can you find out who made it when you get back, and let us know?"

"Be glad to." I paused and downed my glass. Screw sipping. "Took out the Corridor Pack, too."

He let out a slow, high whistle. "Impressive. However, I sense a large 'but' coming."

"But Kara didn't make it—at least, not entirely."

He let out a sigh. "She turn?"

I nodded slowly. "Vampire."

"Sheee-it." He poured me two more fingers of scotch. "I hate it for you, son."

"Thanks, Bernie. It means a lot."

We sat in silence for a few moments, enjoying the whiskey and the cool air, until Bernie broke the calm again. "You know you have to get your shit together for those two kids, right?"

He gave me a fatherly look and waited for a response. When I gave none, he continued.

"After Marge and I realized that chances were slim to none of seeing our kids and grandkids again, we could have fallen apart. I nearly did, but Marge wasn't having it. People had already started showing up around here, and Marge said they needed looking after. So, that's what we did.

"Life in the Marines taught me that you don't have time for pity parties and other emotional bullshit when there's a job to do. And right now, your job is looking after those kids. Sure, they're both tough as nails, but they're following you because of who you are." He raised his glass to me and downed his scotch. "Don't lose sight of that."

I gave a short nod. "Point taken. I won't."

He stood up and clapped me on the shoulder. "Good. Now, let's eat."

After lunch, we politely declined their offer to spend the night, on the excuse that we had someone else to visit and a long walk back to the Facility. They declined my offer to come back to the Facility with us, so I promised to bring back any of their friends who wanted to return, just as soon as I was able. Marge wiped a tear from her eye and kissed my cheek.

"You're a good man, Scratch Sullivan, for bringing them back. Don't ever let anyone tell you any different."

"I appreciate the sentiment, Marge. Hopefully I'll have some company for you, next time I stop in."

She grinned from ear to ear. "Don't make it too long."

"I won't." After an extended goodbye, we headed out in a northwesterly direction. I let Gabby take the lead, as she was the only one who knew where we were headed. A few hours later, we came up on a small, walled settlement. I'd seen it a few times on trips to the Badlands and Corridor, but had never stopped in since their sentries didn't look too friendly. Folks living this close to the Corridor tended to be jumpy, and it just wasn't worth the risk to try to make friends.

Technically, Bernie and Margie's place was in the Badlands, that space between the former safe zones and the Corridor that few people cared to travel. But it was so isolated, I doubted they ever had much trouble before the Corridor Pack came through, except maybe from punters. On the other hand, the settlement Gabby had led us to was on the edge of the safe zone territory. It was still dangerous country, but not so bad that good walls and a few snipers couldn't make it work.

We walked up to the gate in full sight, with the gate sentries' rifles trained on us the whole time. Once we got close enough for them to recognize faces, the guard hollered a welcome to Gabby and let us in.

The person on guard duty was a short, powerfully-built woman with close-cropped hair and a weathered face. "Didn't think we'd ever see you again, little one," she said as we entered the gate. She leaned in and whispered to Gabby as she passed. "I don't think you're very welcome here, despite what you did. My advice is that you don't stay too long."

Gabby gave her a serious look. "I don't intend to, Kate. Thanks for the warning, though. Is Paco around?"

She laughed. "Same place that old coot always is, when he's not tending the pigs." She pointed across the courtyard to a shaded area with rough-hewn benches, where an old Latino man was smoking a pipe. "Where he gets tobacco from is beyond me. We never see him leave the compound, yet he always has a full pipe. Damnedest thing, and if I didn't know any better I'd say he was some sort of magician."

Gabby chuckled. "That wouldn't surprise me. We'll be out of your hair in no time—I just want to say hi to Paco for a minute."

"Sure thing, kid," she answered, before leaning in and whispering again. "Just remember what I said, alright? I don't want any trouble."

I noticed that Gabby had been pointedly ignoring a stocky girl staring at us from the back porch of the main house. "There won't be. At least, not on my part."

As we walked across the yard, a young red-haired boy of maybe ten years of age came running out of the house.

"Gabby!"

Gabby turned with a wry smile on her face as the kid jogged up to us, huffing and puffing with the exertion. For a kid living in the apocalypse, this one sure didn't miss many meals.

"Hi, Raleigh," Gabby said quietly.

He screwed his face up in consternation, but apparently he wasn't good at being mad at people. It wasn't long before he cracked a grin, then grabbed Gabby in a big bear hug... much to her discomfort, based on the look of surprise on her face.

"Hi nothing, Gabby," he said as he let her go and stepped back. "You left without saying goodbye."

One glance at Gabby's body language, and the way the girl on the porch was giving us the evil eye, made it easy to see why Gabby had left in a rush. Her eyes dropped to the ground as she replied.

"I know, Raleigh, and I'm sorry. I just couldn't stick around any longer. I had to find—well, I had things to do."

Raleigh looked over his shoulder at the girl on the porch and stuck out his tongue. "I know Vi chased you off. She told me as much after you'd left. Still, you could have said goodbye."

Gabby chewed her lip. "I hate goodbyes."

The boy seemed to ignore her response, suddenly becoming animated and gesticulating wildly. He looked back and forth at Bobby and me and began chattering a mile a minute.

"Hey, you must be Gabby's friends did she tell you she saved my life from the Boogey Man 'cept it wasn't a Boogey Man it was this thing that ate kids and she tricked it and saved me and a bunch of other kids and it was awesome and she burned the place down and nearly got herself killed and this werewolf broke her arm and was going to eat her but Paco"—he stopped to take a small, quick breath as he pointed at the old man sitting in the shade—"Paco shot the werewolf and he even had a broken leg because he fell down a mountain."

He looked back and forth at us again and stuck his hands on his hips. "Well, aren't you going to say something about how brave she is?"

I looked at our werewolf in residence and chuckled.

"Bobby, methinks you have met your twin chachalaca." Gabby stifled a laugh with the back of her hand. I stuck a hand out to the kid. "I'm Aidan, but most folks call me Scratch. Gabby has saved my skin more than once, so I'm well aware of her bravery."

The old man Kate had pointed out earlier glanced over at me after I introduced myself. He puffed on his pipe and watched us with interest.

Bobby frowned at me before addressing Raleigh. "I'm Bobby." He pointed sideways at Gabby with his thumb. "Gabby's alright, most of the time. She likes weird music, but she's fun to have around." The girl punched him on the shoulder, hard. He rubbed his arm, feigning pain that I know he didn't feel.

"Totally uncalled for! That's two demerits on your quarterly performance report." Gabby reared back to punch him again, and he shied away with his hands up in surrender. "Alright, chill already! Sheesh."

He turned to Raleigh again, whispering and pointing at Gabby from behind his hand. "Anger issues," he stated smugly.

Gabby simply shook her head at him and crossed her arms. "*Pinche payaso*," she mumbled under her breath, which got a rise from the old man.

He called to us from his bench, motioning for us to join him. "Gabby, *mija*, come and introduce your friends." He looked at Raleigh, who was obviously about to feel very left out. "You can come as well, *chavalo*, but please remain quiet and respectful while we speak."

Raleigh nodded with enthusiasm. "I will, Mr. Paco." He whispered to Bobby as we walked over to where the old man was sitting. "He hardly ever speaks to me in English, so he must really want to talk to you guys. Mostly he just cusses at me in Spanish. Hey, do you know what a 'cool arrow' is?"

Bobby nodded. "Gabby calls me that all the time, probably because I'm so smooth and fast."

Raleigh screwed his mouth up and chewed on his lip. "Huh. Maybe the old man likes me after all."

As we sat down under the tree, Gabby made introductions all the way around. "Scratch, Bobby—this is Don Paco, a hunter from Mexico City. Don Paco has helped me out in the past. He's—he's a friend."

I heard Raleigh whispering from my left. "Wait a minute, Paco's a hunter? Oh man, now it all makes sense!" Don Paco gave him a sharp look, which silenced him immediately. I was starting to like this guy.

"Don Paco, this is my friend, Bobby." Don Paco nodded to him. "And—"

The old man cut her off, in the politest manner possible. "And this is Scratch Sullivan, the famous protector of the Central Texas safe zones."

I got up and shook hands with him, and he stood to do the same. His grip was surprisingly firm for a man of his age, although I noticed he moved stiffly, favoring one leg.

"*Mucho gusto*, Don Paco. Any friend of Gabby's is a friend of mine."

He looked me in the eye, noting the old scars over my eye and the fresh cuts and bruises on my face. "Likewise, Señor Sullivan, likewise."

I waited for him to sit again before reclaiming my seat. Gabby sat politely while Don Paco cleaned his pipe out, quietly and carefully repacking it with fresh tobacco before he lit up again. Bobby and Raleigh could barely contain their impatience, and each let out a sigh of relief when the old man spoke.

"So, what brings you to visit, *mija*?"

"*Perros diablos*, Don Paco." He nodded, and listened quietly while Gabby related the story the punter had told us.

After she finished her account, Don Paco blew lazy smoke rings while he considered the information Gabby had shared. He pointed the stem of his pipe at her. "Have you seen these 'devil dogs'?"

"No. We only know what we've been told. But do you think it's possible that punter was telling the truth?"

Don Paco puffed on his pipe, and his eyes narrowed as he nodded slowly. "I have seen these things before—at least, something similar to what this person described. In Central America, they are called *Los Cadejos*, evil spirits in the shape of large black dogs. Very dangerous, very hard to kill. But typically, *El Cadejo* hunts alone. No, what I think you are dealing with is something else—the work of a *bruja*, perhaps."

Bobby raised his hand. "What's a broom haw?"

Raleigh slapped him lightly on the arm with the back of his hand. "I was going to ask the same question!"

Gabby rolled her eyes at them both. "A *bruja* is a witch. In our culture, the word almost always refers to an evil person who messes with the supernatural. The good ones are called *curanderas*, and they usually only deal with herbs, healing, and such. *Brujas*, on the other hand, are known to cast curses and give people *mal de ojo*, the evil eye."

Having grown up hearing my mom's folk tales about *brujas*, *lechuzas*, and the like, I was familiar with the concept—but skeptical. I decided to make sure I understood what the old man was implying. "Don Paco, you're saying that if these 'demon dogs' are roaming around the area, they might be controlled by a human?"

"*Sí*, although you can hardly call most *brujas* human. And if this one is letting her familiars kill indiscriminately, well—she must be a very bad witch. Very evil."

"Great," Bobby replied. "Now we have to worry about the

Wicked Witch of the Southwest coming for us." He wriggled his fingers at Gabby and cackled menacingly. "I'll get you, my pretty, and your little werewolf too!"

I frowned at Bobby, while Raleigh looked around, confused. "What werewolf? I thought Don Paco killed him."

Bobby realized his mistake and tried to cover for it. "It's just a saying, kid, from a movie before the War." This seemed to satisfy Raleigh, and he settled back down to listen to our conversation.

I let out a long, heavy sigh. "Don Paco, if this is really the case, how do we deal with these dogs and the person who controls them?"

He tapped his pipe out on the side of the bench. "My best advice? Kill her, before she kills you."

GNAWED

WHILE DON PACO's advice wasn't exactly helpful, it did shed some light on the punter's tale. At least we knew what we might be dealing with, should we run into the same things the punters were running from. It made me wish I had some silver ammo handy, but supplies had been scarce since we'd left Austin. Half my gear had gotten blown up, and the other half had gotten lost along the way.

And while we had plenty back at the Facility, our supplies would begin to dwindle once we started running patrols and watch duty. We'd have to start making scavenging trips to military installations and outposts to find more guns and ammunition. Either that, or I'd have to take a trip out West to my cabin and dig up some of my caches. Not that I wanted to do that, since I preferred to live off what I could find in the wild; those caches were for rainy day use only, as far as I was concerned. But this might qualify, what with having all the settlers and Colin's group of LARPers moving into the Facility.

After we got everyone settled in and things were running smoothly, we also needed to find a way to take it *back*—all of it. The first step was establishing a base of operations at the Facility. It was a lot to think about, and I honestly didn't have the juice to face it at the moment. After stewing on it for a few minutes, I mostly zoned out as we humped it back to the Facility.

We were ten miles south of the farmstead where we'd spoken with Don Paco when we came across the slaughter.

And a slaughter it was; that was the only way to describe it. Bobby was on point, and he whistled to let us know something was up. Gabby and I hopped off the road and into concealment, where we waited for Bobby to return and tell us what he'd found. He popped out of the woods to my left and called Gabby over from the other side of the road.

Bobby's face blanched, and his voice shook slightly as he spoke. "You guys gotta see this for yourselves."

We followed him south along the road for about a hundred yards. When he stopped, he didn't need to say anything to indicate what he'd found. A fresh corpse was scattered in pieces, all over the blacktop.

Bobby squatted next to the largest piece of the body and pointed out several details. "This is the first one, and there are more that way," he said, tilting his head in a westerly direction. "There are both teeth marks and claw marks on the body—it's been chewed up pretty good."

"Is that our guy, from back at the greenhouse?" I asked.

Bobby nodded. The punter's trench coat was torn to shreds, but the boots were untouched. Jagged white bone and macerated flesh stuck out from a dirty tube sock inside one of those boots. I guessed he'd hauled ass to catch up with his group after I'd let him go, only to get mauled to pieces. He'd have been better off heading the other direction, it seemed.

Bobby walked a few paces away to examine some smaller pieces of the corpse, which included more limbs, the lower half of a torso, and the head—or what was left of it. He pointed around the scene at various bits and chunks.

"Look at this, Scratch. It's all here, every bit of it. Sure, the body is chewed up a lot, and it was torn to pieces, but as far as I can tell nothing's missing. Whatever killed this person wasn't doing it out of hunger."

I looked off into the brush, where I could see a trail of blood and gore that led away from the road. "How many more are there?"

He tilted his head and counted silently on his fingers. "At least a dozen."

Gabby's eyes narrowed and she scanned the area, sidearm already in hand. "Whatever did this could still be around."

I nodded. "Keep your head on a swivel. Bobby, what else are these bodies telling you?"

He shrugged. "Scent-wise, I am definitely picking up a canine odor. But it's muted or altered or something. And there were signs of a struggle. I mean, there are bullet casings everywhere. These punters fought back. But whatever it was that killed these folks? Either the punters took shooting lessons from Stormtroopers, or these things don't bleed."

"You mean to tell me that the only blood you've found is human?"

Bobby stood up and brushed his hands off on his shorts. "That's exactly what I'm saying."

Gabby reacted to that revelation with a pronounced "Huh."

I turned to her and raised an eyebrow. "That mean something to you, kid?"

She shook her head, slowly. "Naw—well, maybe. That thing that Don Paco helped me kill? It didn't bleed, either. You could shoot him, and instead of bleeding he'd leak this black, oily stuff. It was like he was filled with liquid night, you know?"

Bobby and I shared a look. "Funny that this is the first time we've heard about this," he said.

Gabby flipped him off, but her heart wasn't in it as her eyes scanned the trees. "Yeah, well, it's funny that we didn't know you'd been adopted by the Coastal Pack's alpha until a few days ago."

He raised his hands in supplication. "Hey now, no need to get defensive. I'm just saying, it sounds like killing this thing was a pretty big deal. I'm just surprised you never talk about it."

She continued to nervously scan the area around us, looking for threats. "I don't like to talk about it. Truth is, it still gives me nightmares."

Bobby frowned. "Oh," was all he said, as he wisely clammed up for once.

I tapped Gabby on the shoulder to get her attention, and she jumped slightly. "Whoa, settle down, kid. There's nothing around for miles, or Bobby would've heard or smelled it."

She shrugged. "You weren't there, so you didn't see what I saw. And you don't know what these things might be able to do. They could be watching us right now for all we know."

"Okay, fair enough. But I'm curious—how did you manage to kill this thing, if it was so hard to hurt?"

Her gaze continued to slowly pan from left to right. "With fire. I torched that *hijo de puta* like a Roman candle. Then I watched him burn."

We weren't far from the Facility when we found the bodies, so we double-timed it the rest of the way home. About five miles out, Bobby spotted something following us, maybe a mile back as it crested a high ridge. Now, we were the ones being hunted.

We sprinted down the roads and jeep trails of Camp

Bullis, hoping that the pest control system was still working to keep the way ahead clear of any deaders we might have run into otherwise. It was, but the signal frequency generated by the Facility's zombie deterrent system didn't seem to slow these "demon dogs" down at all. I looked back and spotted them on our trail about a half-mile behind us—a group of about two dozen largish animals, loping along together in pack formation.

For some reason, the sight of them reminded me of Cesar the dog trainer. I'd used to watch his show before the War, and seeing the pack of whatever was chasing us made me think of him running along with all the adopted dogs he had on his ranch. But these creatures moved together with a single-minded purpose, like a true pack on the hunt. And they were closing in on us, faster than I might have liked. I reached up and loosened the katana in the scabbard over my shoulder.

Gabby spotted one of the LARPers standing watch. I figured Colin must've started posting them on patrol and guard duty since they'd arrived. Thankfully, it was the kid we'd rescued from that nos' a while back, Christopher. Instead of issuing a challenge, he waved as soon as he recognized Gabby.

She yelled at him without breaking stride. "Run, you idiot! Get back inside now—and you'd better hold that hatch for us!"

Christopher's eyes widened when he saw the huge pack of hounds on our tail. He turned and sprinted for the nearest entrance, a trap door that was hidden under a fake tree stump. Christopher flipped the stump over to reveal a hatch that had been left ajar. It was lazy OPSEC, but there'd be time to bitch about it later. Truth was, his laziness was going to save our bacon.

That chubby kid could move when he had to, that was for sure. Even so, the hounds were practically on top of us by the time Christopher threw the hatch back and dropped down the tube. Gabby went down behind him, and I pushed Bobby into the hole before he could argue. I figured if he broke anything, he'd heal faster than any of us.

As I climbed down the ladder, I paused to spare a glance at the creatures that were in the lead, maybe twenty-five yards away. They were a motley mix of larger dog breeds—Rottweilers, Dobermans, German Shepherds, and the like—along with some hunting breeds and a few mutts. But they were misshapen and ill-formed, mutated somehow into larger, darker things. Their coats were black as night, and each dog had its lips pulled back to reveal slavering rows of unnaturally large teeth. The hounds foamed at the mouth, every last one, and even in the daylight their dead-looking eyes glowed with a dull shine from within, like a wolf's eyes reflect light at night.

But the strangest thing about them was how silent they were on approach. They didn't bark, howl, snarl, or growl as they bore down on me, every eye focused on their prey. Before they closed the gap, I pulled the false tree stump over me and closed the hatch, sealing it tight.

The kids were all sprawled out on the cold concrete floor below, staring up at me with looks of mingled fear and curiosity. I stayed on the ladder and listened for signs that the hounds were outside the hatch. I thought I heard some scratching and sniffing, but it could have just been my imagination. I waited and listened a few more minutes, then climbed down the ladder.

Christopher spoke up first. "What the hell was that? I've seen some wild dog packs before, but nothing like that. What were those things?"

I held a finger to my lips and gave him a stern look. "Ssshh. Not a word to anyone about what we just saw, until I have a chance to speak to Colin about it. Got it?"

He nodded and rubbed his face.

"And put the word out to pull everyone on watch and

from a distance through their familiars, or they use their voice to seduce and control their opponents." I gave him a quizzical look. "Think Saruman or Gríma Wormtongue in *The Lord of the Rings*."

I nodded. "Got it. Like mind control."

"Yes, but much subtler. Generally, it takes the typical witch a while to gain complete control over a victim. It begins with deception, with the witch gaining the confidence of their prey. Then, they gradually get their target to concede more and more of their free will, until eventually the witch has complete control of their prey's mind. But a very powerful witch can turn a weak mind in seconds."

He paused to yell some commands at the students, who were still working on the same drill, then turned back to me with a serious look. "The thing that makes them so dangerous is that they're masters of deception. You could have a witch here in the Facility, and never even know it."

"Sounds serious. What about curses and crap like that? Is any of that stuff in their playbook?"

Colin's face blanched, and he looked away. "Yes, but it's rare. You'd have to be dealing with an exceptionally powerful witch for them to have the juice to place a curse on you."

I remembered something that Piotr had said to Colin when he was greeting us, something about the Curse of Cú Chulainn. I decided against pressing for more info on the topic. Instead, I changed gears.

"So, what do you think about these demon dog things? Any idea what they might be?"

"I'd say they're definitely a threat. The thing the old man mentioned, *El Cadejo*? That's basically the Latin American version of a black shuck or barghest. And he's right; they tend to hunt alone, which leads me to agree with his assessment. I'm thinking these are familiars—dogs that have either been possessed, or raised from the dead to do the witch's bidding."

"As in demon possessed?" I asked.

He nodded. "I have some experience dealing with supernatural animals, and they can be difficult to fight one-on-one... never mind in a pack." He paused for a moment, brow creased in thought. "Maybe we should try to catch or kill one to examine it, so I can see exactly what we're dealing with."

I slapped him on the shoulder. "I like the way you think. Let me track down the Doc and see if she can offer us any help."

He laughed. "Good luck with that. Captain Perez disappeared the day after we arrived with the first group. She makes occasional appearances to boss Nadine and Janie around, then vanishes into thin air again. I still haven't figured out where she's been hiding."

"Gabby will know where to find her. After I speak with her, I'll let you know if she has anything we can use to trap a demon-possessed canine."

He nodded. "Fair enough. Just don't go on any dog catching expeditions without me."

"Oh, I wouldn't dream of it. Somebody has to be the bait for the trap."

GABBY FOUND me before I found her. Her bedraggled appearance told me she hadn't eaten or bathed yet, and from the worried look on her face, I could tell she had bad news for me. The sounds of people arguing echoed at me from the direction in which she'd come. Something told me I wasn't going to get much downtime today.

Gabby jogged up to me and shook her head. "The shouting you hear is Janie arguing with Dame Sweetlove—Anna—over the LARPers not helping out with cleaning and cooking. Anna says it's because they have to be responsible for patrols and security, but Janie says the Facility is plenty secure, and they should be helping out in the mess like everyone else."

I pinched the bridge of my nose and took a deep breath. "Can't we just let them work this out on their own?"

Gabby laughed silently through her nose, then her expression turned serious. "Normally I'd say no, we can't, but Christopher says we're missing three people. He called in everyone who was on guard duty and running patrols, just like you asked. But a patrol and one of the guards didn't make it back."

"Our people or theirs? Wait, scratch that—they're all our people. But were they LARPers or settlers?"

"From what I understand, one LARPer, one from Canyon Lake, and one from Kara's settlement."

I rubbed my beard and sighed, because I'd been looking forward to a shower and shave. "Well, shit. We need to find them. Go get cleaned up and fed, and make sure Bobby does the same. Then, wait for me in the mess."

"Can do." She turned to go.

"Aw, hell. Sorry, Gabs, but I need a favor."

She shrugged. "Sure thing. What's up?"

"I need you to take me to the Doc's lab."

Since Gabby and the Doc had first taken me inside the Facility, I'd only ever been on the main level. But I knew there had to be more to the place. I was no scientist, but even I could figure out that the Doc had to have a lab somewhere. Moreover, I suspected the government had used deaders as test subjects—and if so, they sure as hell wouldn't keep them on the main level.

It was a topic that I'd avoided bringing up thus far, not because I wasn't curious, but because I'd had more pressing matters at hand—not turning into a shambler and rescuing Kara being tops on that list. But I'd been thinking about it since the events in Austin, and knew I'd need to bring it up with them eventually.

Gabby tried to be evasive with me. "I don't know what you're talking about, Scratch," she said, giving me a blank look.

"You're a shitty liar, kid. No, you're a good liar—which is why I don't believe you. Your poker face is what gives you away. So, let's cut the bullshit. Just take me to the super-secret sublevel or wherever the Doc does all her hocus pocus, alright?"

Gabby chewed her lip and narrowed her eyes. "She's going to be pissed. And besides, it's classified."

I laughed so hard I nearly snorted. "Are you shitting me? Look around you, kid—you see any federal agents waiting to lock us up for poking our nose into government secrets?"

She screwed her mouth sideways and frowned. "Just because you don't see them around, doesn't mean they don't exist."

"Gabby, for the last eight years I've been waiting for some remnant of the government to return and rescue us all from this nightmare. And in all that time, not once have I ever seen any evidence that any government infrastructure survived the War and invasion."

She went all stone-faced on me and clammed up. *Huh.*

"That is, unless you know something I don't... aw, who am I kidding? *Of course* you do. Because between you and me and the Doc, I'm always the last one to get the important, earth-shattering news."

The shouting down the hall got louder, and Gabby clucked her tongue. "C'mon, I'll show you how to get to her lab and the containment area—but I'm not going with you. Once I let you in, you're on your own."

I did a double-take at the word "containment." Even though I'd suspected it, it was still a shock to find out I was right. "Containment area? Never mind, I'm sure I'll find out when I get there."

Gabby led me down several corridors into an area of the Facility that was rarely used. After checking to make sure we hadn't been followed, she opened a false panel that concealed a keypad, into which she entered a twelve-digit combination. A section of the wall swung back, revealing descending stairwell.

She gestured toward the door. "Hurry up, before someone

comes. I'll shut the door behind you. Aunt Lorena will have to let you back out again."

I shook my head. "You two and your secrets."

Gabby gave me an indecipherable look, and shooed me with her hands. "Hurry, before anyone sees! I'll find Bobby and meet you in the mess hall when you're done."

"Kid, you, me, and the Doc are going to have a long talk—very, very soon." I sighed and headed through the door and down the stairs, with the whine of hydraulics and whoosh of an airlock echoing behind me.

The stairs continued down several more flights, but the placard on the wall at the first landing said "Research Sublevel 1," so I went through the metal door to see what I could see. The layout and decor were similar to the level above: mid-century bomb shelter. The walls were painted in an ugly light green color, and the concrete floor was sealed and polished. The hall I was in led straight ahead and to the right. I chose to go right at random, figuring I'd backtrack if I didn't find the Doc.

The hallway was lined with windows, and behind those windows were a multitude of labs, complete with chemistry analyzers, work stations, refrigerators, hundreds of glass beakers and test tubes, Bunsen burners, microscopes, centrifuges, and the like. It was shocking, seeing a place that was this clean and sterile, when the world outside was anything but. There were also offices down here, all of them dark and devoid of life. I walked past the labs and empty offices until I turned a corner to another hallway, identical to the one I'd just left.

Midway down that hall, I found the Doc in a lab. Why she was working in that specific lab, I hadn't a clue, because they'd all looked the same to me. She had her eyes glued to a microscope, and was taking notes on a pad off to the side as she worked. I depressed a button next to the door, a six-inch aluminum square like they used to have in office buildings next to automatic doors. The glass door slid to the side with a whoosh, and I walked into the lab.

"I was wondering when Gabby was going to spill the beans," she said, without looking up from her microscope.

"Well, you have to give the kid some credit, because she did play dumb for all of sixty seconds before she cracked."

The Doc made a few more notes on the pad, then removed a pair of latex gloves and tossed them in a wastebasket close by. She stuffed her hands in the pockets of her lab coat and gave me an inscrutable smile.

"Sadly, she's unable to say no to just about anything you ask. Normally I'd discourage that sort of hero worship, but for the most part you've been a positive influence on her."

I looked around the lab, taking it all in. "You know I wouldn't do anything to hurt her, Lorena."

"Hmmm... I believe that's the first time you've addressed me by my first name." She pursed her lips. "Don't make a habit of it. I need to maintain an air of authority around here, now that you've brought all these strays home with you."

"If I'd have thought about it, I would have suggested that you pin some birds on your collars, just for the added effect."

She rolled her eyes. "You know as well as I do that these people would be in awe of any officer in uniform, regardless of their rank. But I doubt my superiors would appreciate it if I brevetted myself in order to impress a few civilians. Just letting them inside this facility is enough to get me court-martialed as it is."

I took a deep breath and let it out slowly. "Before you give me the grand tour, how about you fill me in on just who your 'superiors' are, and how in the hell there's still a chain of command left after all this time."

"My superiors are members of the U.S. government and military who went underground before the bombs fell. When the invasion started—well, they opted to remain hidden to ensure a continuity of government, just in case things really got out of hand."

"Lucky them. So, if this remnant of our government still exists, why haven't they organized and sent out the cavalry to save our asses?"

She reached back and adjusted her ponytail, pulling it even tighter than it already was. "Mostly because they simply don't have the resources or people to pull it off. After weighing all our options, command decided that the project I was involved with, as well as a few other R&D projects, held the most promise for eventually giving us the ability to defeat Them.

"Scratch, the reality is that there's only a few hundred people, government and military, left in installations like this one across the country. We remain in contact via satellite communications, but as the orbit of those satellites decay and we lose them one by one, our infrastructure is breaking down. Not only that, but some of our installations have been infiltrated and destroyed."

"Thus, the secrecy."

She nodded. "Exactly."

"So, you're taking a huge risk by letting these settlers in here."

"A calculated risk, actually. Until now, I didn't have a serum that was stable enough to test on a broader basis. Oh, it's been coming along over the last eight years, but slowly. That is, until I started running tests on the blood samples I took from you before you left for Austin."

She paused, then pointed to a nearby stool. "You may want to sit down for this."

"I'll stand, thanks." The Doc shrugged and sat down, leaning an elbow on the counter as she did so.

"Scratch, you were selected as a test subject for this project, before you got injured. Back in Afghanistan, you and several other subjects were exposed to an inert version of the deader virus, in the hopes that your body would develop antibodies or a resistance to the pathogen that could be used in research to develop a vaccine at a later date.

"None of the other test subjects panned out. Not a single one developed any immunity whatsoever to deader venom. However, it seems something was triggered in your immune system after you were bitten and exposed to Bobby's blood. What I'm saying is that it's not the serum that's fighting off the infection in your body—it's you."

To be honest, I didn't know whether to be angry or grateful. Uncle Sam had a history of experimenting on service members without their knowledge or consent, but I thought that shit had ended with Tuskegee. Apparently, it hadn't.

Should I have been surprised? Not really. Uncle Sam could give two rat turds about a soldier's civil rights, the Uniform Code of Military Justice be damned. I mulled over what the Doc had said for a few moments, then decided it wasn't worth being upset about. Especially not if it had saved me from turning.

"Alright, Doc, let me get this straight. When I was in the service, I was selected for this project of yours—"

"Project Cerberus," she interjected.

"Right, Project Cerberus. After that, I was given an inert

form of deader venom—probably something they snuck into a vaccination, like they did with the anthrax vaccinations in Desert Storm."

"Correct. In fact, that was the first stage of the serum trials on humans. Soldiers who didn't get sick or die after receiving the inert deader venom were advanced into the next stages."

"But after I got injured and was sent home, I was deemed unfit for the project."

She shook her head. "Not necessarily. You could have still participated, but at the time we were looking for completely whole and healthy candidates. So, your jacket ended up in the alternates pile."

"I guess your standards must have dropped, what with the zombie apocalypse and all." She didn't even blink. "So, my next question is, what happened to all the other candidates?"

The Doc tsked and tapped her lips with a knuckle. "Let's see—some candidates refused to participate. Several more exhibited less than desirable psychological traits and washed out before receiving the treatments. Two test subjects died from adverse reactions to the serum. Four subjects completed the trials successfully. One was assigned here, to protect me and this installation. He disappeared on a mission not too long ago."

A lightbulb went off for me, and something clicked into place. "Gabby's mysterious Uncle Tony, I presume."

"Yes, that's correct."

"And the other three test subjects?"

"One was KIA during the invasion, and the other two are assigned to different installations. I am unaware of their activities at the present."

I ran through a number of questions I wanted to ask, but I didn't want to push her too hard. So, I skipped ahead to the one thing that was tops on my "I need to know right now" list.

"Alright, that clears up some loose ends for me. Now, show me the containment unit."

I followed her out of the lab and down a corridor, through a keycard-protected metal door, down a hall, through another door that opened with a keypad, and into a room with a large bank vault-style door. She gestured at the vault.

"The containment area."

"Impressive. Now, show me what's inside."

The Doc's face was blank. "As you wish," she replied, and walked over to a panel next to the door. She entered another lengthy code into a keypad and the vault door hissed, clanked, and slowly swung open.

"How do you know there's not something wicked waiting for you on the other side?" I asked.

"Because the vault door wouldn't open if there were."

I nodded. "Huh. So what happens in case of a complete power failure?"

"Total lockdown. Nothing gets in or out of this vault under those conditions."

It took several seconds for the door to open all the way, after which I followed her through the entrance. The room beyond was mostly steel and concrete, with a series of large metal shutters covering what I assumed were enclosure observation windows, in rows along either side of the room. Safety tape had been placed on the floor in front of some of the enclosures, demarcating a safe viewing distance, I presumed.

I whistled, long and slow. "Wow, the military spared no expense on this place, did they?"

"After a few early incidents, the powers that be decided it

was in their best interests to ensure the absolute security of any supernatural entities in their possession."

"Don't you mean 'custody'?"

"I meant what I said. The government sees these things as property, and nothing more."

I thought about the repercussions of having werewolf DNA spliced onto my own, and how that might affect my civil rights and citizenship under a functioning government. I also thought about Bobby and Gabby. I made a mental note to get the three of us really lost, really fast, should we ever end up with a functioning government again. No doubt they'd have us locked up and then throw away the key, once we were no longer of use to them.

Still, I couldn't see that happening in my lifetime. The best-case scenario was that we'd dose a couple dozen of our people with the serum, and then we'd push the deaders, vamps, and anything else that wasn't mostly human out of the Texas Hill Country. As far as I could see that was the most we could hope for, all things considered.

The Doc spoke and pulled me out of my reverie. "What you see before you are ten state of the art containment units, constructed out of a special alloy that contains both iron and silver. The observation windows are made from an extremely high-tensile-strength polymer, capable of withstanding .50 caliber gunfire. Each containment unit is outfitted with a number of countermeasure devices, including anesthesia, silver nitrate and acid mist nozzles, and flamethrowers. Also, the walls, floor, and ceiling of each unit can be charged with high-voltage electricity."

"Does that work?"

She shrugged. "Different methods work on different supernatural species. Obviously, silver works best on weres and vampires. Acid works well on zombified humans because it melts their connective tissue. Electricity works on deaders as well, but only momentarily. Fire works on pretty much all of Them."

Before tussling with the Corridor Pack, I'd never used fire against the creatures, simply because it was impossible to control the aftermath. If you started a fire and it spread, you might just end up burning down your safe house or cutting off your only avenue of escape. Besides that, brush fires could be deadly in the safe zones, which was why almost every settlement cleared brush and cut fire breaks before the dry season.

However, it was a weapon worth exploring. I made a mental note to come up with a reliable way to manufacture Molotov cocktails. Heck, there might have even been some Willy Pete grenades or a flamethrower lying around. I'd get Gabby to help me search later, after I dealt with the Doc.

"How many of these units are currently occupied?" I asked.

She smiled a wicked grin. "All of them. Most of our test subjects are kept in a sort of suspended animation. We reduce the level of oxygen inside the cells, and keep the temperature at subzero levels. Even the dead need some oxygen for their cells to function, and for the most part all living matter slows down the colder it gets. The combination keeps most of Them dormant, or at least unable to cause us much trouble."

I nodded, impressed at the setup. "It's too bad we couldn't find a way to use that method offensively."

The Doc checked some data on a computer screen as she replied. "We tried coming up with a weapon that could freeze them, but the tech just wasn't there. Grenades, guns that shot liquid nitrogen—none of it was reliable enough for field use."

"Hey, you said that low oxygen levels and extreme cold worked on 'most' of Them. You mean you have one in here that's awake right now?"

"Yes, that's correct. Let me introduce you to Subject 217."

I FOLLOWED the Doc over to a cell halfway down the row on the right side of the room. She hit a button on the wall and I heard the clank of a lock releasing, then the metal shutter over the observation window slid up with an electronic whine. The space beyond was dark, and there was condensation on the glass.

I leaned in to look more closely, and noticed that what I was seeing wasn't condensation; it was a spider's web. Then, a face unlike anything I'd ever seen before slowly advanced into the light. The thing's mottled skin was chitinous, yet pliable, and covered in tiny hairs. It had multiple pairs of dark, shiny eyes on its face and forehead, above and below two larger orbs that stared at me from where a human's eye sockets would have been. Perhaps strangest of all, the creature had a split lower jaw, bifurcating into mandibles that ended in sharp black fangs that dripped saliva... or venom.

It moved closer to the glass, observing me with those creepy eyes. The thing had a humanoid body, with the exception of two pairs of spider-like appendages that extended from either side of its torso under it's more human-looking arms. It was also naked, and had teats running down either side of its torso, like a female dog or pig.

"What—what is that thing?"

"As far as we can tell? It's a *Jorōgumo*, a form of *yōkai*—Japanese demons. How it ended up here in the U.S., we don't know. It's the only one we've ever found. When it was captured, it had taken the form of a beautiful Japanese woman who was working as a prostitute near Houston. Oil field workers and refinery employees started going missing, and when their desiccated corpses began showing up, we got wind of it and sent in a team to investigate. We lost three top-tier operators capturing it, and we've been studying it ever since."

"I'll be damned. It's a freaking were-spider?"

I tapped the glass, and the thing cocked its head at odd angles in response, those unblinking eyes glued to mine. Then, it began to morph, changing its shape and transforming into the most beautiful Asian woman I had ever seen. She had milky white skin that was unblemished and flawless, and long flowing black hair that cascaded down her shoulders, barely covering her absolutely perfect breasts. She moved seductively behind the glass, and I found that I couldn't take my eyes off her exquisite nakedness. As I watched her hips sway and her firm, heavy breasts undulate, I heard a voice inside my head.

Free me, and I am yours, it said. *Forever.*

I stood there for a moment mesmerized, then began looking around for some way to release her from her cell. That is, until the metal shutter slammed down over the enclosure observation window. I was left standing there with a very embarrassing bulge in my pants, wondering what the hell had just happened.

The Doc crossed her arms and tapped a finger on her chin. "Hmmm... I honestly didn't think she'd take an interest in you. Sorry about that. I figured you weren't her type."

I coughed and turned away in embarrassment. "Well, this is awkward."

The Doc chuckled. "Oh, don't sweat it. She used to do that to most of the guys in the lab. Nearly caused an escape incident once, so they stopped letting the men work with her. I ended up doing all the research on her after that."

She paused and pointed at my nether regions, twirling her finger around. "It's sort of like supernatural Viagra. It'll take a while for that to go away."

I let out a small sigh. "Thanks for the warning. Next time, I think I'll skip the tour and just ask for a status report."

"Oh, get over yourself. I'm a scientist, Scratch. You think we didn't run tests on her abilities, to see if there was a way we could replicate her telepathy? Trust me, I've seen a lot stronger reactions than that to Jori, as I like to call her."

I removed my BDU jacket and sat down in a chair nearby, covering myself with the clothing—much to the Doc's amusement.

"So, did your research turn up anything that could be of use?"

The Doc's face was a blank slate as she responded. "No, I can't say it ever did."

"Huh. Seems like a lot of effort, keeping her alive here and all if she's not of any use."

She busied herself at a nearby workstation and avoided making eye contact. "Well, the decision was made to keep her alive, on the odd chance that we might find a way to tap into her abilities at some point."

I knew I was onto something, but I didn't know what. Still, the fact that I'd just been humiliated made me want to pursue this line of questioning further.

"But did you ever try to concoct some sort of super-serum from her DNA? I mean, surely you brainiacs and the powers that be considered it. I figure the CIA would just love to have a bunch of mind-controlling Mata Hari's running around, seducing foreign diplomats and stealing state secrets. Heck, that's a spook's wet dream, no pun intended."

She continued to busy herself at the workstation, avoiding eye contact with me. "We did," she said, "but it never panned out."

"Huh. Too bad, I suppose." The Doc never was much on conversation, but based on her reticence, it appeared that I'd hit a nerve. I looked around the room for a moment, and decided to change the topic of conversation. "Hey, it looks like I'm going to be stuck here while I wait for things downstairs to go back to normal. You got anything to read?"

An hour later, I headed back to the main level, still embarrassed but decidedly ready to forget that I just been brain-raped by a were-spider. We still needed to look for our missing people, so I quickly showered and headed to the mess hall for a bite to eat. Gabby and Bobby were there waiting on me, playing cards and drinking instant coffee like a couple of old folks sitting around a nursing home.

I walked by them on my way to see what was in a big pot on a table out front. Whatever it was, the smell of it had my stomach growling from all the way down the hall.

"You guys hear anything about our missing folks while I was gone?"

Bobby didn't bother looking up from his cards as he replied. "Nope, nothing. You sure you want to go out looking for them now? It's getting kind of late. Might be better to wait until morning."

Gabby rolled her eyes. "Bobby, we're the only people here

who can see in the dark. Stop being such a baby." He stuck his tongue out at her, and she grabbed a card from the discard pile, expertly throwing it hard enough to stick in his forehead.

"Owww! Damn it, Gabby, I told you if you did that again I was going to stop teaching you how to play cards." He plucked the card from his forehead and wiped the blood away, and the small cut stopped bleeding almost instantly.

She looked at me and smirked as she laid her hand face down on the table, then she stabbed a finger in Bobby's direction. "Dog boy here says he's scared of puppies."

"Say what?" I scratched my head. "How in the hell can you be a werewolf and be afraid of dogs?"

"See there? That's just bigoted thinking. Can't a werewolf have a simple phobia? Big-ass dogs make me nervous. I have my reasons, so can we just leave it at that?"

I shook my head. "You're shitting me, right? I mean, not too long ago, we fought a wolf the size of a small pony. I didn't see you shying away from that fight."

He slapped his cards down on the table. "See what I mean? Bigoted, the both of you. We fought a giant *wolf*, w-o-l-f. Not a giant dog. And certainly not a pack of them with shiny eyes and teeth that would give Jaws nightmares. Giant wolves, I'm fine with—but demonic dogs? Not so much."

"So, what about Ghost? You sure weren't afraid of him. Speaking of which, where is that dog? Didn't they bring him from the castle house?"

Gabby smirked and laughed. "He says that one dog wasn't a big deal, but getting chased by a pack of hounds freaked him out. And yes, Ghost is here, but Janie wouldn't let me bring him in the mess hall."

"Well, I suppose there must be rules."

Her eyes narrowed. "Sure, but it isn't exactly fair." She pointed at Bobby again. "He gets to come in here, but Ghost doesn't? That's not fair. Ghost is way cleaner than Bobby, and he leaves less of a mess after he eats, too."

Bobby gave her a dirty look. "Just because I got a little excited about finding a can of Natural Balance Duck and Potato dog food, it doesn't mean that I'm a slob."

"Oh no? You had flecks of that stuff all over you. It was in your hair and everything."

Bobby crossed his arms and sat upright in his chair with his nose in the air. "I'm not playing cards with you anymore."

"Baby."

"Loser."

"Wimp."

I walked off while they were still arguing, and grabbed a bowl from the table. I picked the pot lid up and peered underneath. *Menudo, yum.* Smelled like crap when you cooked it, because you were cooking intestines. But boy, was it delicious. I betted dimes to donuts it was Janie's doing. I got a bowl and scarfed it down, and by the time I finished, the kids were still going at it.

"Alright, enough. You ready to go find these things?"

Gabby made a face and chuckled. "Well, I am—but the wittle baby here is probably worried he's gonna get bitten by a puppy dog."

Bobby decided to give her the silent treatment.

"Oh, are you going to cry, wittle baby?"

Bobby was starting to fume. I decided to step in. "Gabby, that's enough."

She ignored me and kept it up. "What's wrong? You worried the hounds might use you as a chew toy?"

I could see that Bobby's nails were growing longer, and his jawline was shifting. "Gabby, get up and walk away from this table, right now." My voice was low and clear, and it startled her out of her tirade.

She looked at Bobby, then at me, then back at Bobby with a surprised look on her face. "Okay, geez—I didn't mean anything by it. We joke around like this all the time."

I looked her in the eyes. "Go. Now."

She pushed herself away from the table. "Alright. I'll be waiting by the exit hatch."

After she was gone, I waited a few minutes for Bobby to calm down. "So, you going to tell me what happened?"

He took a deep breath and looked away. "My parents got killed by wild dogs, after the bombs fell. That's messed up, right? It wasn't the bombs or the zombies that got them. It was a mangy pack of mutts."

"I'm sorry, Bobby. I had no idea."

"Well, it's not something that comes up often in conversation. 'Hey, nice machete—and oh, by the way, my parents got eaten by dingos."

"I guess not. No, I guess that wouldn't normally come up in conversation."

He shifted in his chair and worked some kinks out of his shoulders. "That's how I ended up on my own. We were out here from California visiting relatives, and then the bombs fell. We got out of the city and found an abandoned house to hide in, way out in the ranch country, down south near the coast. Middle of nowhere. We thought we were safe, and we were for a long time. They left me by myself while they went out to look for some food, but they never came back. I went looking for them, and found their bodies a few days later, surrounded by bloody paw prints. The only way I could recognize them was by my dad's shoes."

"That's horrible, kid. If I'd have known..."

"Don't beat yourself up over it. When I came across those bodies today, it didn't really bother me then. It was only later, when I had a chance to think about it, that it hit me. That was what my parents experienced, right before they died."

He took a swig of coffee and wiped a drop off the side of his cup with his thumb. "The dogs don't bother me, not really. But the memories do."

I stood up and clapped him on the shoulder. "Stay here, and chill out for the evening. I'll get Colin to come along instead. The three of us are more than capable of handling it."

He looked up at me with glassy eyes. "You sure?"

"I'm sure, son. And the next time something like this comes up, I want you to talk to me, okay? Believe me, I have my own demons, and I know what it's like to be haunted by your memories."

Bobby wiped his nose with the sleeve of his t-shirt, stretching it to reach his face. "I will."

"Good. We'll be back in a few hours." I stood and turned to go.

"Scratch?"

"Yeah, kid?"

"Tell Gabby I'm not mad at her."

I stopped and considered it for a moment. "I think she knows."

I posted guards at all the exits to the Facility, then Colin, Gabby, and I headed out. I chose an escape hatch that was well away from the entrance we'd used earlier, just in case. We spent a good five minutes listening at the hatch before I opened it, and I wished the Facility had electronic surveillance aboveground. They had, once, but the EMP from the bombs had fried the cameras and no one had bothered to replace them.

I made a note to scavenge for some working cameras,

another item on a long list of things that needed to be done to make this place a permanent home for the group.

All was quiet outside, except for the usual night sounds and the wind whistling through the trees. We headed to where the missing guard had been posted, looking for signs of a struggle. What we found instead were human footprints leading away from the guard's post. From the look of it, she'd been standing guard when something had caught her attention, so she'd decided to investigate. *Alone.* The kid was brave, but stupid.

I looked at Colin and whispered. "One of yours?"

He shook his head. "Naw, one of the people we rescued from the Pack. I think she said she was from Canyon Lake? Volunteered to stand guard, said she wanted to help protect the group."

"And you let her?" I asked, trying to keep the accusation from my voice and failing.

Colin scowled at me. "Well, it's not like I'm in charge around here—at least not as far as the settlers are concerned. I can keep my boys in line, but every time Anna, Mickey, and I tried to organize the rest of them, Nadine undermined our efforts in some way. I got tired of dealing with her, and figured I'd let you handle it when you arrived. So, the settlers have pretty much been doing as they please."

"I still don't understand why you didn't assign one of your people to pull guard duty with her."

"Honestly? Because I didn't think it was necessary. We haven't seen a shambler within a mile of this place since we got here. Security wasn't really a concern, at least not until you led those dogs back here—good job on that, by the way. After security, a shortage of food has been our main concern, so I've had my boys out hunting wild game to keep everyone fed."

"I still say it was negligent to let the girl come out here alone," I hissed.

"And I say... you know what? Fuck you, Scratch. You've been pissy ever since you found out your girl got turned into a vamp. Guess what? I've been doing this shit a hell of a lot longer than you have, and it happens when you're in this business. Nothing you do can change it, so I suggest you quit taking your guilt out on everyone else."

Colin and I glared at each other until Gabby stepped between us. She glanced at each of us in turn as she spoke, her voice low but hot with impatience. "Scratch, Colin is right—you're being a *cabrón*. And Colin, Scratch is right—that girl had no business being out here alone. Now, can we get back on task? Arguing isn't going to help us find our people."

Gabby's words were sufficient to put us both in our places. "Gabby has a point," I said. "And I had no right to question you. I'm sure it's been difficult, holding things together these last few days. I'm just on edge about this situation. The Facility was supposed to be a safe haven for us."

Colin cracked his neck and exhaled forcefully. "I think we're all under a bit of pressure. No one's had a chance to take a break since we tangled with the Corridor Pack. I for one was looking forward to getting a breather, but instead it's been nothing but worry since we got here. No offense, but I think a lot of people in our group are having second thoughts about teaming up with you."

"I'm sure that's mostly due to Nadine's influence." I ran a hand through my hair. "Look, I'll deal with her when we get back—after we find out what happened to our missing people."

Colin nodded. "Fair enough."

Gabby was already heading off into the brush, following the trail the guard had left. "Kiss and make up later, *pendejos*. We have work to do."

GABBY FOLLOWED the girl's trail through the brush, live oaks, and juniper, and Colin and I tagged along silently as we avoided looking at each other. Truth was, I liked the guy, and I felt bad about giving him a hard time. Besides, he was the closest thing I'd had to a friend my age since the bombs had dropped and the dead risen.

Was he mysterious? Yeah, because I'd seen him do some weird stuff—like sneaking up on me, for instance. No one snuck up on me, but somehow he managed to do it, and that alone told me he was more than he appeared. But did it mean I didn't trust him?

Hell no, because he'd stuck by the LARPers when he didn't have to, and he'd stuck his neck out for us when we'd fought the Corridor Pack. As far as I was concerned, the guy was alright. I wasn't used to all this friendship business, but based on past experience I figured he was a dude, and he'd get over it quick. Hell, if we'd have slugged it out, we'd probably have been laughing and joking right now. Sometimes, guys just needed to let off a little steam, and throwing a few punches was often the best way to do it.

A grunt from Gabby pulled me back to the present. "Scratch, look at this."

She pointed at a spot where the ground had been disturbed, indicating that our missing girl had changed direction rapidly. She'd started running, and not only that—she was being chased by a pack of canines.

We picked up the pace, letting Gabby take the lead since she was likely the best tracker of the three of us. A hundred yards farther we heard a gunshot, and a female voice yelling and cussing.

"Get away from me, you mutts. Go away!"

I signaled to Gabby and Colin to stick together, but to come around from the other side. As they snuck off, I checked the AK-47 rifle I was carrying, to make sure I had a full mag and one in the chamber. Then, I crept silently forward, closer to where we'd heard the girl's voice.

About thirty yards on, I came to a small rise, and the girl's cussing became more distinct. I dropped to my belly and crawled forward until I could just barely peek over the top of the hill. Up ahead, five large black dogs had an Asian girl of about sixteen or seventeen treed in a large live oak.

She was well up in the branches, higher than any of them could leap or climb, but a rangy pit bull mix was making the effort. It'd take a run at the main trunk, scramble up several feet, and try to get its front paws over a limb. I watched it try and fail several times as I waited to make sure Colin and Gabby were in position.

Along with the bully, I saw an Australian Shepherd mix, a Dobie, a lab, and some sort of heeler. Any one of them was plenty big enough to rip the girl to shreds.

The hounds were completely focused on the girl, who was trying to climb higher in the tree. I wanted to shout at her to stay put, because if she climbed any higher I doubted the branches would hold her. She shimmied farther up the trunk to reach for a limb, then slipped, dropping her rifle to the ground below. The girl held on by one hand, her feet dangling in the air only eight feet or so above the eerily silent pack of dogs beneath her.

Time to see what hurts these things, I thought. I sighted in on the bully's head and squeezed the trigger. It dropped like a rock, tumbling to the ground where it remained still. I was hidden in the brush, but it wouldn't take the hounds long to zero in on my position. I decided to take a few more out, when something weird starting happening with the pit bull.

The dog kind of wobbled to its feet, and stood back up.

What the hell?

I'd seen a lot of weird shit, but I'd never seen a deader, ghoul, revenant, or vamp take a bullet to the head and get back up. Well, maybe I'd seen a vamp or two take a couple of bullets to drop them, but I'd never seen one bounce back like that after they'd been dropped. A 'thrope could, though; you could blow their brains out, and they'd heal up in a few minutes or more, depending on how old and tough they were. Really, the only way to drop a werewolf was blowing them to smithereens, or beheading them.

And if that was the kind of weird we were dealing with here, then I needed to move quick before that kid's grip gave out. I broke from concealment firing, hoping like hell that Colin and Gabby were in position already. I walked toward the pack, calmly and carefully taking head shots at each, dropping them one at a time.

My shots were answered by two more rifles from the brush on the other side of the tree at my two o'clock. Within seconds, all the hounds were on the ground, although a couple were starting to twitch. I slung my rifle and drew my katana, then I ran at the Dobie as it was starting to get up.

Cold steel flashed in the moonlight, and the hound's head

flew off into the dirt nearby. I breathed a sigh of relief as the hound's body collapsed and lay still.

"You gotta behead them, or they'll come right back to life!" I shouted.

Gabby and Colin took the hint, and soon they went to work —Gabby with her kukri, and Colin with that sword he always carried. Moments later, the hounds were headless and bleeding thick, dark blood in the dirt. The way they bled just didn't look right, though. It was like their blood had started to coagulate in their veins. It was nearly black, deoxygenated, and it oozed instead of draining out of them.

Not only that, but they smelled like the dead.

What the hell are these things? Zombie hounds? Dog ghouls? I hadn't a clue, but based on the look on Colin's face, I was about to find out.

"I'm about to drop, so you better move out of the way or catch me—your call," the girl yelled from above me.

I moved out of the way, because I knew better than to try to catch a hundred and ten-pound teenager falling out of a tree. She let go of the limb and plummeted, hitting the ground with a drop and roll that would have made any airborne ranger proud. I reached out a hand to help her up, but she ignored it and reached for her rifle instead, looking it over and checking to make sure it still functioned.

Once she was satisfied that her firearm was serviceable, she turned to me and stuck out her hand. "Name's Tam, but most people call me Tammy."

"I'm Scratch, and this is Colin and Gabby."

She nodded at Gabby, who returned her nod. Colin was

busy examining the hounds, so Tammy gave him a shrug and turned back to me.

"I know who you all are—I think everyone in the group does, after that rescue you pulled off back in Austin."

"You hear that, Scratch? We're famous," Gabby joked.

Tammy smiled shyly. "Anyway, thanks for coming out here after me. I tried shooting them, but you saw what good that did." She paused and nudged the nearby corpse of one of the dogs with the toe of her boot. "After seeing a couple of them come back to life, I decided to save my ammo. Speaking of which, what the hell are these things? Never seen anything like them, not even when we got captured by the Pack."

"I'm... we're not sure yet. We got chased by a bunch of them on the way back from Austin. I called everyone in from patrol and guard duty when we got here, just in case. We heard you and a few others were missing, so we came looking for you."

She wiped her nose with the back of her sleeve. "Yeah, the patrol. Did you find them yet?" I shook my head. "Damn. I heard gunshots and went to investigate. I saw some dogs chasing two boys and took a shot at them, thinking it'd scare them off. Five of the pack broke off and started chasing me, which is how I ended up here. You think the dogs got them?"

"Maybe. Let's go find out," I said, trying to keep my voice neutral. Colin stood and wiped his hands on his pants. I caught his eye over Tammy's shoulder, and he shook his head slowly. Whatever he'd discovered, it wasn't good. "Gabby, lead the way."

She headed off wordlessly toward the direction we'd come from, and the rest of us followed her. Forty yards beyond, where Tammy had changed direction after the hounds had begun chasing her, we found the bodies of the two who'd been on patrol. One of them was a LARPer, and the other a woman from Kara's settlement.

"Oh, Ethan, you poor soul," Colin muttered.

The big swordsman knelt next to the remains of the boy—or at least the largest piece, which was a torso with the head and most of one arm still attached. He laid a hand on the boy's head and closed his eyes for a moment, silent. Then, he marched off into the brush and began chopping saplings down with his sword. I caught Gabby's attention and inclined my head in Colin's direction. She split off and started helping him lash tree limbs together to make a litter.

Tammy walked over to the other body, a mangled mess of flesh and bone. "Did you know her well?" I asked.

"Naw, not really. I mean, we were together with the Pack on the research campus, but they kept us separated most of the time and didn't let us talk much. Her name was Olivia, I think."

The name didn't ring a bell, so I squatted down and brushed some hair away from her face. *Shit.* I recognized her from the settlement, back when this whole thing had started. I'd saved her from a trio of punters who were going to rape her in front of her kid. Or her and the kid both. I wasn't sure.

One of them had been Pancho Vanilla, who'd escaped that encounter and then caused us no end of misery thereafter. He'd recently received his just desserts, and at my hands. It angered me that I'd saved this Olivia lady from punters and the Corridor Pack, only to have her die out here, chewed up like some dead animal. I wondered who'd look after her little girl, now that she was gone.

Just when I thought we were making progress, or that we'd be safe, some new nightmare would rear its ugly head and prove me wrong.

Damn it to hell. Damn it all to hell.

Colin and Gabby finished their task, and we silently began the bloody work of gathering what was left of Olivia and Ethan.

We would lay them to rest properly after we got back to the Facility.

Rather than risk another attack by the dogs, we put the remains in body bags until we could be certain it was safe to bury the dead properly. The Doc assured me she had a safe place to store them in the meantime. Word of the loss spread silently through the group, putting people on edge or in grieving all around the Facility.

Colin and I sat in the mess, sipping cheap vodka out of a pair of tin cups he'd produced along with the bottle. He had a habit of coming up with stuff out of the blue, but I wasn't about to question him over it. I took a slug of the white liquid, and savored the burn as it went down.

"So... you going to tell me what you found out there?"

He stared in his cup and swirled the contents around a bit. "Ethan was a good kid. Hell, I practically raised him."

"Been a while since you lost someone?" He nodded. "I seem to be making a habit of it lately, and I'm getting damned tired of it."

He looked up at me, raising his cup. "To the fallen."

I clinked my cup against his. "To the fallen," I echoed. We downed our vodka, then he set the cup on the table and clasped his hands together.

"Scratch, how much do you know about magic?"

It was an odd question, and it threw me off a bit. Don Paco had hinted at it, what with the talk of witches and all, but I was skeptical—to say the least.

"You mean, besides the dead rising, vampires and were-wolves stalking the earth, rabbi alchemists, flesh golems, and all the other crazy shit I've seen?" I shrugged. "Not much, and to be honest, I never really thought about it. Killing Them only requires that I accept that these things exist. If you ask me, spending too much time on *why* they exist... well, that way lies madness."

He tsked. "I can respect that, although I'll say that after hunting... *them* for a few decades, I've learned that having intel on your enemy often makes the difference between living and dying. Especially where the supernatural is concerned."

I considered his point as I poured us more vodka. "Can't argue with that, I suppose. Truth is, up until recently I rarely ran across any creatures that were more intelligent than wild animals. Oh, I'd occasionally get the odd nosferatu who could speak, but you don't get much deep conversation from a nos'. Mostly I dealt with revs, ghouls, and the like. Not much intel to be had there, other than 'head shots work' and 'beheading works better.'"

He pursed his lips and took a sip from his cup. "So, you don't think there's something behind everything that's happened?"

"I didn't say that. Back at the nuclear lab, I saw something through that... hole in reality that Piotr made. If I had to describe it, it was a look into hell. There were things over there that wanted to get over here. And they were hungry."

Colin nodded. "What would you say if I told you that was just one of many alternate dimensions inhabited by evil entities? There are things beyond imagining, Scratch, and they want nothing more than to rip through the fabric of time and space to get here, so they can destroy everything."

"Seems to me like some of them already did exactly that," I quipped.

"Well, sort of. Supernatural beings were here already, though, long before the apocalypse happened. But creatures like Piotr's maker, and that giant wolf we killed, Vánagandr?

They're what we call primaries. They can't really be killed, per se. And although you can destroy their physical form, they'll eventually come back, perhaps decades or centuries later."

I took a slug of vodka. "Seems a bit farfetched to me, brother."

Colin chuckled. "But vampires, zombies, and werewolves aren't. Right."

I tilted my head and rubbed the stubble on my chin. "I suppose you make a good point."

He tapped the table with his index finger for emphasis as he continued. "All I'm saying is, there are powerful things out there, and often they're trying to bring more of their kind over here, from wherever they came from. Why? Mostly because they're evil, or power hungry, or just plain *hungry*. And they want what we have, because compared to their worlds, ours is a paradise."

"If you don't mind me asking, how is it you came to believe all this stuff?"

"Like I told you back at the castle house, I've been fighting *them* for years, long before the shit hit the fan. I know it because I've seen it—hell, I've seen shit you couldn't imagine in your worst nightmares."

I decided to withhold comment. As far as I was concerned, the less I knew about the crazy world Colin and the Doc played in, the better. Plus, I still wasn't ready to buy into what he was selling. Oh, I believed that he believed it, but personally I could care less about all that mystical bullshit. Since the dead had risen, my only curiosity about the supernatural was limited to, "Does it want to kill me?" and "Then how the hell do I kill it?"

Keeping things simple had kept me sane for eight long years, and I wasn't about to change my outlook at this juncture. The whole conversation was getting just a little too weird for me, so I decided to get us back on task. I leaned back in my chair, kicking my feet up on the table as I interlaced my fingers behind my head.

"So, what's this got to do with our undead dog problem?"

"Magic caused it. Whoever this witch is that's raising these familiars, she's using necromancy to create them."

"You mean like raising the dead and stuff? Look around, Colin. That's nothing new."

"You don't understand. People who deal in necromancy are bad news. When we run into her—and believe me, we will, eventually—I have a feeling she's going to be a pain in the ass to put down."

"Okeydokey, noted." I took a moment, to make sure I wanted to ask the next question. "Colin, are you a witch of some sort?"

He raised an eyebrow. "Do you see me wearing a pointy hat?"

"I'm serious, man. Let's just say for a minute that all this magic stuff is real—not that I completely accept that, but let's just say it is."

"I assure you, it's real."

"Sure, whatever. If you can do magic"—I wiggled my fingers in the air—"and we're going to be facing something that can use magic... well, seems like it'd be helpful to know someone on our team can fight fire with fire."

He cracked his neck and stretched, arching his back with a yawn. "I'm beat. Think I'm going to turn in."

"Fine, ignore the question then."

He stood and regarded me with hooded eyes, then looked around the room to make sure no one was within earshot. Colin placed both hands on the table and leaned in.

"Look, Scratch, I've found that most people have gotten used to the idea of zombies, 'thropes, vamps, and the like. But they also like their humans nice and normal, so they can maintain a neat and tidy 'us and them' worldview. There's just no middle ground for most folks these days. Either you're one of *them*, or one of us."

He paused as he clenched his hands into fists. "But consider this. I kept a group of kids alive and safe for years, living right next door to a pack of bloodthirsty 'thropes." He stood and pushed his shirtsleeves up to his elbows. "So yeah, I've got a few tricks up these sleeves. And when the time comes, if it means keeping my people alive, I'll damned sure use them."

He walked off without another word. After he'd gone, I grabbed the vodka bottle and poured some on the floor.

"To the fallen," I muttered.

BEGIN

ONCE COLIN LEFT, I mulled over things over until I decided our next steps. After seeing how hard those deader dogs were to kill, I knew the safety of everyone at the Facility would be compromised by their presence. And the fact that whoever was making them could just make more? That had me really worried.

Colin was pretty adamant that there was a magic user involved—whatever the hell that meant. *Why couldn't things have stayed nice and simple? Why couldn't this just be a normal zombie apocalypse, with nice, slow-moving deaders, and a mall full of food, guns, and ammo to hole up in?*

It seemed like the whole world had gone batshit crazy. Not like it hadn't been before, but ever since that nos' had tipped me off about the coming incursion, things had *really* gone off the deep end. Witches were raising possessed hounds from the dead —or possessing them to raise them from the dead... I still hadn't figured that one out. We had a spider demon in the basement, and who knew what else the Doc hadn't revealed. Hell was trying to tear a hole in the fabric of reality, so they could bring more of Them over here.

And the icing on the cake? Finding out my girlfriend's a vampire, and I'm a government lab rat. Yeah, good times.

But this was no time to wallow in self-pity and hopelessness. After three combat tours and eight years fighting Them, I knew things could get even more FUBAR in a heartbeat. All it'd take was one slip, one breach in security, and we'd be dog meat.

Which meant it was time to go on the offensive. And I figured that if I was going to deal with the current mess, I'd better take the knuckleheads with me... if only to keep them out of worse trouble than I was about to get into.

I found Bobby and Gabby listening to some pre-war music in one of the offices. I vaguely recognized the tune, if you could call it that, since it was mostly just screams and power chords. Not exactly my thing, but I could understand the appeal.

As I walked in the room, Gabby was banging her head and beating a rhythm on the side of a metal trash can in time with the music. Bobby had his fingers in his ears, while Ghost had his ears covered with his paws nearby.

"Do you think you could play that a little louder?" I asked. The sarcasm in my voice was lost on the kid.

"Yeah, isn't it great?" Gabby shouted. "It's the Sex Pistols! Colin loaned it to me."

Bobby looked a lot less impressed. "I prefer my sitar music," he said with a shrug.

Gabby was still banging her head when I shut off the music. "Hey, why'd you have to do that? 'God Save the Queen' was up next. I like that song!"

I pinched the bridge of my nose as I replied. "It was giving me a headache. Anyway, we need to talk."

She flipped the trash can over and set it down, then took a seat on the edge of the desk. "Sure thing, Scratch. What's up?"

"We need to do something about the deader dogs. So long as they're a local presence, the Facility is compromised. Not only do they pose an immediate threat, but they could also lead other things right to us... things that are far worse."

Gabby scratched deep lines in the desk with her Kabar as she spoke. "Don Paco said there'd be a *bruja* or *brujo* controlling them. So, we find and kill the person responsible, and take care of the problem at the source. Seems pretty straightforward to me." She stabbed her knife into the table and punched her palm.

"Bobby, what's your take on the situation?"

While Gabby was all for taking the bull by the horns, for once Bobby's face showed concern. "I think we oughta lead them away—you know, draw them off and then take them out if we can."

Colin's voice echoed from the hall. "Not a bad idea, but you'll still have to deal with the witch. Whatever her familiars see, she sees. Which means that eventually, you'll have to go after her, too." I looked over my shoulder to find Colin leaning in the doorway. "Sorry, I was passing by and couldn't help but overhear your conversation. Anyway, the real question is, what does she want?"

Gabby frowned at the big swordsman. "How do you know it's a she?"

He shrugged. "Powerful witches are almost always female. Sure, it could be a warlock or magician, but my hunch says it's a she."

Bobby scratched his head. "And what makes you an expert on witches and stuff?"

"Colin was a hunter before the War," I said. "You spent years with the Coastal Pack, Bobby. Didn't they ever mention that supernatural creatures existed before the shit hit the fan?"

Bobby nodded. "Sure they did—but it's not like they held history classes or anything. Every once in a while, you might hear an old-timer talk about life before the War, but mostly we were just focused on the Pack's survival. Samson taught me how to control my lycanthropy, but as far as other creatures were concerned, he only told me how to avoid them or kill them."

Colin nodded. "That sounds like Samson. He never was much of a conversationalist."

Bobby did a double-take. "Wait a minute—you know Samson?"

Colin chuckled. "I did, before the War. Glad to hear he's still around. I take it he's the alpha of the Coastal Pack?"

Bobby nodded. "Yep, despite more than a few challengers over the years. He kind of took me in and raised me after my parents died."

"Was it his idea to turn you, or yours?" Colin asked.

"That's Pack business," Bobby stated. "Can't discuss it."

Gabby had begun carving up the desk again as she listened. "This is all very educational, but we were talking about how to deal with the demon dogs..."

"I vote we call them deader dogs," Bobby interjected.

"*Ay, lobo chiflado...* who cares what they're called? I just want to know how we're going to get rid of them."

"I'll answer that question," I said. "We're going to lead them away from here, just like Bobby said. Then, we're going to lose them. And when they give up on catching us, we'll follow them back to their maker."

Colin tracked me down later, while I was prepping for our little excursion. "I noticed you avoided the question about what this witch might want."

I kept loading magazines while I considered how to answer. I'd snagged an M4 from the armory—which thankfully was still locked up—and every spare mag I could get my hands on. I'd also spent time making a shit-ton of silver-tipped hollow points for my sidearm. If we had to tangle with a pack of those things, I wanted to be ready.

I slapped a full mag on the desk and grabbed another. "I didn't necessarily avoid it. I just didn't want to get into it in front of the kids."

"They're hardly kids, Scratch. Not after what they've been through."

I thumbed a few more rounds of 5.56 in the magazine I was loading. The repetitive motion seemed to help me think, and made me wish I had more reloading supplies here at the Facility. Nothing was better for keeping your hands busy while your mind wandered than reloading a few thousand rounds over several hours.

"They've seen a lot, sure. But they're still kids."

Colin tsked. "If you say so. But I wasn't much older than Gabby by the time I was hunting things way worse than this witch's familiars. You're not helping them by withholding info."

"I am if it keeps them from getting killed by disobeying an order." I put another full mag on the stack, counting the total in my head. *Three hundred rounds. Not enough.* I paused for a moment, then stuck my head out the door and looked up and down the hall before I shut the door to the armory. "Look, I've already given a lot of thought to the motive behind these dog attacks. When the time comes to face whoever's behind it, I don't want the kids tagging along and getting killed... or worse."

"You think the Dallas Coven is to blame?" I nodded. "What do you think their motive is?"

I reached into my breast pocket for a pack of cigarettes that wasn't there. I'd run out since we'd arrived, which meant I was going to suffer until I could scrounge up more. With nothing else to do with my hands, I opened another box of rounds and dumped a few in my palm, then started loading an empty magazine.

"Revenge, maybe... or keeping us occupied while they continue what Piotr was working on. Hell, I don't know exactly. It's just a little too convenient how these things showed up, right after we took out Piotr and the Corridor Pack."

Colin leaned back against the wall and crossed his arms. "You think this witch was sent by the Dallas coven? That maybe she's looking for you?"

I loaded another round. *Click.* "Actually, I figured you'd know better than me whether that was the case. I've never had to deal with the vamps up in Dallas, and if I had my way I'd keep avoiding them like the plague. You're the expert on all things supernatural, so you tell me."

He cradled his face and rubbed his chin stubble with one hand. "Honestly? It's not just possible; it's highly probable. Whatever Piotr was attempting to accomplish in Austin, I suspect it was important to the coven. Since you screwed it up for them, it wouldn't be a stretch to think they'd want revenge. Vamps are assholes that way. But the thing that worries me most? Most vamps are bloodthirsty as all hell, sure... but I've never known one who wanted to see the earth burn."

I set a half-full mag down on the desk. "Hell, I just figured they wanted to feed on us—you know, use us as cattle and what-not."

Colin shook his head. "If that were the case, they'd have wanted to keep more humans alive. Unleashing an undead apocalypse didn't exactly leave a lot of humans alive to feed on. Decimating the population just doesn't make sense."

"You're sure the vamps were behind the outbreak?"

He cleared his throat. "Almost positive. Scratch, do you know how zombies and ghouls are made?"

I started loading again. "Beyond someone getting bit? If you're asking if I know how the first one was created, I never much thought about it. Figured it happened in a lab or something."

Colin gave a grim smile. "If only. There are only three ways to make a zombie or a ghoul. The first and most obvious is for a human to get bitten, just like you said. They get infected, and then they turn."

"Old news. Tell me something I don't know."

"Alright then, here goes. The second way to create a zombie is with magic—necromancy. Raising the dead by animating their corpses, much as I suspect this witch has done to create these familiars."

"And the third way?"

"Getting drained by a vampire, but not turned completely."

I stopped loading and looked at him. "No shit?"

"No shit. It's actually damned hard for a vampire to make another vampire. They have to feed on each other, then the master vamp has to time everything just right so the perfect amount of vyrus gets in the subject's body..."

"Virus? Vampirism is caused by a virus too?"

Colin wavered his hand back and forth. "Sort of—and it's 'vyrus' with a 'y.' Yes, it's a contagion, but of the magical kind."

"Aw shit, here we go again."

The big swordsman looked at me with one eyebrow arched. "Hey, believe me or don't. All I'm saying is that, for this outbreak to happen all at once all over the world, either multiple vamps or multiple necromancers had to be behind it."

I finished loading the last magazine and placed it on the stack. *Lucky thirteen. Three hundred and ninety rounds.* It'd have to do. Damn, but carrying it all was going to be a bitch. I'd have to get Bobby to help me pack horse the other gear, because I really preferred to keep the extra rounds on me.

"Well, that's kind of jacked up," I said matter-of-factly.

Colin shrugged. "It might be worse."

"Oh yeah? How?"

"We could be dealing with a vampire who's also a witch."

"Is that bad?" I asked, wondering what could be worse than a creature like Piotr.

Colin chuckled humorlessly. "Damned straight. Take the most powerful undead creature in existence, and give them the power to raise and control the dead at will... shit, I don't even want to think about it."

"Have you ever tangled with one before?"

He kicked off the wall and shook his head slowly. "Witches? Sure. But a vamp who could raise the dead? Hell no. And if you and I are lucky, we'll never have to."

We headed out early the following morning, leaving the Facility and all its current inhabitants under the watchful eyes of the Doc, Anna, and Mickey. We left an obvious trail for the deader dog pack, knowing full well that once we had them in pursuit, it was going to be a race for our own survival. For that reason, I let Bobby carry most of the gear, figuring that I'd need to move fast to keep from becoming puppy chow.

Two hours later, the deader dogs had picked up our scent. They were, of course, eerily silent. The only way we knew they were following us was because Bobby was pulling rear guard. When he came running up on us at werewolf speed, we knew the game was on, so we hauled ass toward our intended destination.

My plan was to lead them several miles southeast of Camp Bullis and the Facility, to the once heavily-populated outskirts of north San Antonio. My bet was that the suburbs and commercial areas around Loop 1604 and Highway 281 would be crawling with deaders. And, I figured that we could use their scent and movement to confuse the deader dog pack until they lost our trail. We'd hide out and observe them from an elevated position, then we'd follow them back to whoever had been making the damned things.

It was a simple, straightforward plan with few moving parts. Run like hell, don't get eaten, and follow the bastards back to the source. *Piece of cake.*

Or, at least, it would have been—except for one thing. As we headed into a neighborhood just a mile or so outside Camp Bullis, Gabby was the first one to point out the error in my plan.

"Where are all the deaders?" she asked between breaths as we ran down an empty, somewhat overgrown suburban street.

She was right; there weren't any deaders around. I'd expected to start seeing a few stragglers or small groups by this point, but there weren't any to be seen anywhere.

"Shit," I gasped. "Just keep moving. We'll run into some eventually."

They did exactly as I asked, and we kept running through the neighborhoods of north central San Antonio. Unfortunately, even though we were well inside the boundaries of one of the most densely populated areas in South Central Texas, we didn't see a deader once. Not a single soulless, rotting, walking corpse.

But what we did start seeing were body parts. Or, more specifically, dismembered deaders. At first, it was just a random body part here and there—but the further we ran, the more I realized my mistake.

It wasn't just living humans these deader dogs had been attacking. They'd been taking out the deaders too. And apparently, we'd run right into their hunting grounds.

"Bobby, how far back is that pack?"

The werewolf looked back, squinting his eyes. "Lead dog is roughly one hundred yards behind us, and closing."

"Um, Scratch?" Gabby said, as she pointed ahead of us and

to our left, at a gap between a couple of commercial buildings in a strip mall. "Look."

It was another pack of deader dogs running parallel to us, moving into position to box us in.

Colin spoke up from my left. "There are more on our other flank, and gaining fast."

I looked to our left and behind us, and hell if there wasn't another, smaller pack shadowing us from the other side of the highway. *Damn it.*

"There must be fifty of them, at least," Bobby said, his voice getting higher with stress. "What are we going to do?"

I looked around the area as we fled, searching for a way out of the trap I'd led us into. "We're dead meat out here in the open. New plan—find higher ground, something with choke points we can defend." I pointed to a tall building nearby. "There, that hospital. Go!"

Bobby and Gabby changed course, heading for the multi-story building I'd pointed at, while I drew my sidearm and started shooting on the run, plugging holes in hounds that got too close. Colin produced a pistol from somewhere—I had no idea where, since he hadn't been carrying one earlier—and began taking hounds out with careful aim.

I knew they'd simply heal and get back up again, but that didn't matter right now. All we needed to do was clear a path to the hospital. From there, we'd make it to an upper floor, then barricade the stairwells to keep the hounds out. That'd give us time to figure out an exit strategy.

I looked back to see that the three smaller packs had now merged into a single, loping mass of canine fury that was nearly nipping at our heels. As I fired random shots behind me, Colin pulled something from his jacket. It was a beer bottle, of all things. Fluid sloshed inside, and the tip was stuffed tightly with a cloth wick.

"Molotov?" I shouted.

The big swordsman nodded. Somehow, he managed to light the thing. I couldn't see how, because I was too busy shooting hounds that were trying to cut us off. He tossed the bottle over his shoulder, and I watched it arc through the air and land in the midst of the dogs behind us. It shattered on impact, lighting half of them on fire and scattering the pack.

"Nice work, David Blaine," I huffed.

He chuckled and wheezed his reply. "They'll regroup soon —only bought us a little time."

I shot two more of the big black dogs and watched them tumble away from us. We ran on, following Gabby and Bobby through the parking lot of the hospital to the emergency entrance.

THE GLASS ENTRY to the emergency department had been shattered, but I wasn't concerned about that. Glass wouldn't hold those things back anyway. We needed to put some concrete and steel between us and them.

"Look for a stairwell," I shouted, hoping that the final occupants of this building hadn't barricaded themselves in from above.

Bobby took the lead, following signs that indicated the way to the elevators. As we ran down hallways filled with desiccated corpses—the non-moving kind—I turned over crash carts and gurneys in hopes of slowing the pack of black dogs down. It was pretty much a wasted effort. The creepy bastards jumped over everything I threw at them like they were running schutzhund or something.

I shot a wolfhound right between its pale, glowing eyes as it skidded around a corner behind us. The clicking of nails on the tile floor was the only indication that more were coming. Lots more, in fact. The sound reminded me of a horror movie I'd once seen, where a swarm of scarab beetles overtook some unlucky soul and picked his bones clean. The sound effects used in the movie had sounded a lot like the noise made by the pack as they pursued us through the hospital.

"Bobby, find us an exit, now!" I yelled.

"I am, boss, I am—there!" He ran to a metal doorway that was marked "stairs," and tried the latch. Whatever was behind it, it was locked or jammed tight. Bobby backed up and made as if he was going to bust it down.

"Don't!" Gabby yelled. "If we break it, they'll have the run of the stairwell, and we'll still be screwed."

I searched around frantically, then saw a possible exit. "Bobby, open the doors to that elevator shaft, now."

The kid looked at me like I was crazy, then he grinned. "Ah, we're going to do a John McClane—good thinking, boss."

Bobby shifted form just enough to get some claws on his fingertips, then forced his fingers into the gap and began pulling the doors apart. The space between increased to a few inches, then a foot, then two. The werewolf wedged himself in between the doors and pushed with all his might until the doors were wide open.

The clicking noises were getting closer. I unslung my rifle and set up on one side of the elevator doors, and Colin on the other. I tossed him my Glock, figuring he'd need the extra firepower.

"Look for the pit ladder," I said. "Rungs built into the wall of the elevator shaft. Gabby, jump on Bobby's back." She gave me an exasperated look. "Just do it!"

The kid jumped on Bobby's back, wrapping her legs around his torso and her arms around his neck. The werewolf didn't need to be told twice what to do—he leapt into the elevator shaft and disappeared into the darkness above, just as the first hounds appeared.

Colin and I both started firing at once, dropping undead dogs like flies, only to have two or three more scrambling over the bodies of each one we shot. The noise from the gunfire was deafening, standing in sharp contrast to the silent, undead animals we were fighting. I missed a dog as it jumped at me, and was saved as a clawed, furry hand swiped it out of the air with a solid crunch.

Bobby was standing there beside me, in his full 'thrope form. Colin was still firing away on the other side of the door—then I heard silence.

"I'm out!" he shouted.

I fired a few shots past Colin, while Bobby pushed me toward the elevator shaft. "Scratch, go," he growled. "I got this. I'll hold them off until you guys are free, then I'll follow after."

I hesitated, because even in werewolf form the kid's voice was all nerves. Before I could protest, he picked me up by my shirt collar and belt and tossed me across the elevator shaft. I crashed awkwardly into the side wall, barely managing to catch myself on a rung of the pit ladder. Soon I saw Colin flying at me, so I swung myself to the side and grabbed at him with a free hand while my rifle clattered into the shaft below. Colin managed to grab a rung, and soon he was climbing up the ladder.

I hung in place, watching Bobby cussing, ripping, and tearing at the pack of undead hounds as they attacked him from all angles. I pulled my pistol and fired at the damned things, but it did little good. Soon, the kid was nearly pulled down by the weight of the pack, and I watched as he stumbled backward and fell down the shaft.

"Bobby—no!" I yelled as I watched him fall away into the darkness, still clawing and snapping at the undead dogs who had latched their jaws onto him as he fell.

Colin called to me from above. "Scratch, c'mon. There's nothing you can do for him, and trust me, he'll be fine. He's a fucking 'thrope, for goodness' sake. It'll take a lot more than a short fall and a few mutts to do that kid in."

I peered down into the complete darkness below, and although I could hear sounds of fighting, I couldn't really see a damned thing. I looked at the open elevator doors nearby, where the remaining hounds stood silently watching us from just a few feet away. A shaggy German Shepherd mix with a matted coat jumped at me and I batted it away, causing it to bounce off the wall and tumble into the darkness.

Above, Colin was already climbing toward an opening one story up. Wisely, I decided to follow him, writing off my rifle —and all the ammo Bobby had been carrying for me—as a loss. I looked back as I climbed, only to see a dozen or more pairs of glowing yellow and red eyes staring back at me in the gloom.

"Where's Bobby?" Gabby asked as we crawled through a narrow gap, squeezing through a pair of elevator doors just beneath the permanently stalled elevator cab above.

Colin answered her, since he was the first one through the doors. "He stayed behind to cover our exit."

Without hesitation, Gabby lunged at the doors just as I was coming through, but Colin stopped her with an arm around her waist. "Relax, he'll be fine. Unless those things have silver-coated teeth, I doubt they'll be able to do enough damage to slow him down. Trust me, I've known a lot of werewolves in my time, and they're damned hard to kill. He'll be along shortly, don't you worry."

I rolled over onto my back, catching my breath as I hugged my arm to my side. My bite was aching like a son of bitch, and in the back of my mind I feared I'd start having seizures again from the venom. I pulled my shirtsleeve down to hide the gangrenous venom trails around my bite, then pushed myself to a seated position against the wall.

"You sure he'll be okay, Colin?" I asked.

"As I can be. Hell, you've dealt with 'thropes recently, and you saw how hard they are to put down. It took high explosives and a twelve-story fall to take out most of the Corridor Pack. A twenty-foot drop and some zombified pups aren't going to slow your boy down much."

"Why do I get the feeling you know something about Bobby that we don't?" I asked.

Colin looked down at me and shrugged. "Full disclosure? I think there's a reason why Bobby isn't with the Coastal Pack."

I raised an eyebrow. "Can you be more specific?"

"The kid has 'alpha' written all over him. Sure, he kowtows to you because he practically worships the ground you walk on. But he's a natural alpha if I've ever seen one. The way he shifts, it's like it's second nature to him. Not many young 'thropes can do that, Scratch. The kid is a hell of a strong werewolf, and my guess is that he left his Pack to avoid clashing with Samson."

I stretched my neck and sighed. "So, Bobby's not the average bear—er, werewolf?"

Colin sucked on his teeth and shook his head. "Not by a long shot."

"Alright, but if he doesn't show up soon, I'm going after him," Gabby said, her eyes challenging either of us to disagree.

"I promise you, if he doesn't come crawling out of that elevator shaft, I'll beat you to it." I stood and looked around. "Now, let's clear this floor and make sure there aren't any surprises waiting for us."

A quick circuit revealed nothing more than a few dried up deaders that were standing around in a holding pattern. We quickly eliminated them using swords and blades to conserve ammo, then took stock of our situation. Clearly, we were momentarily safe from the undead hounds a floor below us, but we had no idea whether the other stairwells were secure. It looked like we were going to be staying some time, so our second order of business was making certain we wouldn't be ambushed in the night.

"Colin, why don't you and Gabby check the stairwells on the south and east sides of the hospital, and I'll check the north and west sides. Let's meet back here in fifteen minutes."

I watched them leave, then headed off to check my sectors, passing by the elevator doors on the way. Just as Colin had said, Bobby was sitting next to the doors when I walked up. He was bleeding from multiple bite wounds, but alive.

"You look like shit, kid. I don't suppose you happened to bring my rifle with you, did you?"

"Sorry, I was a little distracted, what with bleeding out and all." He paused and smiled. "Hey, Scratch, you know what? I think I got over my wild dog phobia."

I chuckled. "Age and time tend to give you a different perspective on your childhood fears. Well, that and becoming a full-grown 'thrope." I dug around in my pack and pulled out a bundle of jerky and some hardtack. "Good job saving our asses, by the way. I have to go check the stairs, so while I'm gone, eat up so you can heal up."

I tossed the food to him, and he caught it with a wince and a wave. I headed down the hall, finding the northwest stairwell door. I listened at the exit before opening it, and snuck downstairs to see whether it was open or sealed up tight. Thankfully, the door was closed, and a pile of office chairs and hospital gurneys were wedged tightly against the door and frame. No chance the dog pack could reach us that way.

For shits and giggles, I leaned out over the stairwell banister to get a good look through the wire-reinforced door window. Several pairs of yellow and red eyes stared back at me from the other side. I assumed that meant the deader dogs were guarding each of our potential exits, and couldn't help but think there was a higher intelligence guiding their actions.

I went back upstairs and found Colin and Gabby conversing with Bobby, who was already leaking less blood and looking much better.

"Northwest stairwell is secure. What about the other exits?"

Colin spoke up first. "Locked up tighter than a nun's undies. We're safe, for the moment."

I nodded. "I saw deader dogs camped out in front of the northwest exit. You?"

Gabby stopped conversing with Bobby to answer me. "A half-dozen or more. You think they'll still be there in the morning?"

"I'd say the odds are good. But let's not worry about that now. We'll sleep on it, and come up with a way to make our escape in the morning."

As it turned out, the solution found us in the dead of the night. Several hours later, I'd just changed watch with Bobby and was drifting off to sleep when he roused me.

"Um, Scratch? We got company."

"Of what sort?"

"Well... just follow me." The kid led me to a row of broken windows overlooking the east parking lot. He pointed across the lot, to a line of trees on the other side of the hospital helipad. "There, you see them?"

I squinted to make out several shapes in the moonlight, just inside the tree line. "They look human. Are they punters?"

"Actually... no."

I turned and looked at the kid. "Bobby, what aren't you telling me?"

He rubbed the side of his face and looked at the ground. "Well, you know when I got bum-rushed by all those deader dogs? And you remember how I fell down that elevator shaft?"

"How could I forget?"

"Yeah, I guess I kind of freaked out and put out a distress signal through the Pack bonds when that happened."

"What do you mean, 'Pack bonds'?" I asked.

He took a deep breath and let it out slowly. "It's kind of like telepathy, but a lot subtler. When you belong to a werewolf pack, you get these feelings whenever someone in the Pack is experiencing strong emotions. I guess it's like a survival mechanism or something, so the rest of the Pack can help if one of us gets in trouble."

"So, what you're telling me is you sent a telepathic distress signal to the Coastal Pack, and they hauled ass out here in response."

"Yup, that's pretty much what happened."

"So, why aren't they storming the place already?"

He sniffed and rubbed his nose with the back of his hand. "Well, I felt their presence when they got close, so I signaled that I was okay and that they should hang tight and wait."

"Okay." I thought for a moment. "Bobby, are these wolves friendly, or are they like the Corridor Pack?"

"Um, on a scale of one to ten—one being Mr. Rogers, and ten being rabid, cannibalistic 'thropes?"

I ran a hand through my hair. "Sure, let's run with that."

"Well, I'd say maybe a five or six? We don't eat humans, but we're not exactly friendly with them, either."

"You never did explain how you got separated from your Pack."

He glanced out the window. "Nope, I never did, did I?"

"Care to explain?" I asked.

"You know they can hear everything we're saying, right?"

I nodded. "Figured as much. Now talk."

He looked at me, then out the window. "Not here."

I followed the kid down the hall and into an interior room that had once served as a break room for the floor nurses. Bobby sniffed the air as we walked in, looking this way and that.

"I smell food," he muttered, rifling through the cabinets.

His search revealed a metal tin of Danish cookies, probably the only food in the place that hadn't been ravaged by vermin over the years. The kid sat down at a nearby table and popped the tin open, then stuffed a few cookies into his mouth.

"Mmmm... stale but tasty." He tilted the tin toward me. "Want one?"

"Sure, why not?" I grabbed a cookie and nibbled on it. They were nastily stale, to be honest, but not as bad as hardtack. "So, tell me about your family troubles."

Bobby popped a couple more cookies in his pie hole, then started speaking. "Alright, so you know my parents got killed by wild dogs, right? Well, I was only eight or nine at the time. We'd driven out from Santa Cruz to visit family on the Gulf Coast, and while we were on vacation things went to shit."

"Go on," I said between nibbles.

"After my parents got killed, I just sort of hid from the deaders and wild dogs, and did my best to survive. We'd been staying in a resort town just north of Corpus Christi, out on one of the islands. At first, I tried to stay in town, closer to supplies and food. It didn't take long before looters and deaders caused me to head farther down the island, where the rich people had lived.

"I scrounged food and water from condo units, avoiding shamblers and people for months. After a while, the living people got fewer and further between, and the deader population grew. Pretty soon, I was the only living person left on the island, or close to it. I got lonely, so I went looking for survivors.

"Long story short, I got chased out a two-story window by a bunch of shamblers while scavenging for food at a resort hotel. Broke both my legs and my left arm—bones were sticking right out and everything. Good news was that I fell on top of a carport, so the deaders couldn't get to me. Bad news was I went into shock from blood loss, and started fading in and out of consciousness.

"As it turns out, Samson saw the whole thing happen. He and a couple of other 'thropes had escaped to the coast after the bombs fell, and they were just roaming around trying to survive like anyone else. I guess he felt pity for me or something. I remember him saying if he didn't turn me, I was going to die. Said it had to be my choice.

"I said yes, not knowing what I was agreeing to, and he turned me. Savaged my body to do it, worse than it already was —and after I turned he had to break my bones again to reset them so they'd heal properly. Later, he explained that attacking me was the only way to get enough of the 'thrope vyrus into my bloodstream. I asked him why he didn't just spit in my wounds, and he laughed and said, 'Way of the Pack, kid. Everyone goes through it.' He also told me that not everyone makes it when a 'thrope tries to turn them. I made it, so they took me in."

He paused to toss a couple of cookies in his mouth. "Still doesn't explain why you're no longer with the Pack," I said.

"Well... you know how teenagers rebel at a certain age, and clash with their parents?"

"Yeah, all kids do it to an extent."

"Well, with me and Samson it was much worse. We nearly came to blows, on more than one occasion. I finally realized that my behavior was undermining his authority, and if I stuck around he'd either have to put me in my place, or..."

"Or you'd have to beat him and take his place."

Bobby nodded. "So, I left."

I sat and thought about the current situation. "You think your buddies can help us get the hell out of here?"

The kid grinned ear to ear. "Does a wolf shit rabbit fur?"

WHILE COLIN and Gabby were still asleep, Bobby jumped out a second-story window and snuck out to the woods where the Pack was hiding. I'd asked him how they'd gotten from the coast to San Antonio so quickly, and he'd said "motorcycles." I'd asked him where they got fuel, and he'd just said it was "Pack business" and refused to talk about it.

The plan was to have the Pack attack from one side, and us from the other. I stayed up, both to keep watch and just in case something went sideways and the wolves decided to leave us stranded. I'd told Bobby to tell the Pack to attack a few hours after dawn, but just before sun rose, I watched as a dozen large, furry humanoids charged toward the hospital.

"Ah, shit." I ran to where Colin and Gabby were sleeping and woke them both up with a whistle.

Gabby rolled to her feet, pistol in one hand and kukri in the other. Colin, on the other hand, merely laid in the hospital bed he'd chosen for his bunk and looked at me.

"Relax, Gabby—we're not in any imminent danger. At least, I don't think so. Long story short, Bobby's Pack arrived last night, and they're going to help us get out of here."

Colin chuckled and rolled over, covering his head with a pillow. "Yay. Wake me when the slaughter is over, alright?"

Gabby kicked his bed. "Don't you want to go help them? I thought they were your friends, or something?"

Colin's muffled voice replied from under the pillow. "They don't need our help for this. If any vamps show up, let me know. Otherwise, I'm going back to sleep."

"*Pendejo*," Gabby muttered.

"*Entiendo español perfecto, niña*," Colin replied. "And I resemble that remark."

Gabby was about to lunge at him when I stepped between them. "Chill out, Gabby. I know you're concerned about Bobby, but I have a feeling Colin's right. Let him sleep. But just for grins, let's head downstairs and see if we can lend a hand."

"You're just going to be in the way—but sure, do what you want," Colin mumbled.

Gabby flipped him off, then laced up her boots and strapped on her gear. I could already hear the sounds of battle echoing up from the floor below. We descended to the ground level using the pit ladder in the elevator shaft, but by the time we arrived the fight was nearly over.

The werewolves had cut through those evil creatures like a scythe cutting wet grass. Dead, dismembered hounds lay all over the place, and a powerful rotting stench filled the air. Apparently, most of these hounds had been dead for some time, but their animation had stayed their decomposition. Now, those corpses were showing signs of rapid deterioration and decay. It was one of the strangest things I'd seen since the dead had risen... and I'd seen a lot.

Bobby loped up to us in werewolf form. "It'd be best if you guys waited here," he growled. "It's not smart to be around a bunch of strange werewolves right after a battle. You should probably give them a few minutes to settle down."

The kid loped off again, so Gabby and I decided to crawl the rest of the way down the elevator shaft to search for my rifle. Using a disposable lighter as a weak light source, I found it at the bottom of the shaft under a pile of rotting dog corpses, covered in goo and filth, but otherwise serviceable. I'd have to field strip it and clean it thoroughly. Unlike Russian rifles, AR variants weren't known for running flawlessly while dirty.

"I should have kept the damned Kalashnikov," I muttered as I slung goop off the rifle's receiver and stock. We were picking our way back to the ladder when Gabby noticed something.

"Scratch, what the hell is that?"

I strained to see what Gabby was pointing at in the nearly complete darkness. My vision had been enhanced by the Doc's serum, but it only worked in low-light conditions, not complete darkness. I pointed my lighter in that direction, and the faint light revealed a hole a few feet across that had been dug into the concrete wall of the elevator shaft, where the wall met the bottom of the shaft.

I tiptoed across the floor, trying to avoid stepping in any more goo than was necessary, and knelt down to look inside the hole with the lighter. Something had scratched or clawed its way through several feet of concrete, and I could see a tunnel had been dug in the dirt beyond that.

"What the actual hell?" I whispered. Then, I saw the bones. Human bones. "Shit. Gabby, head back up the ladder, now. Go!"

She did as I asked and I followed after her, hoping that whatever had dug that tunnel hadn't been disturbed by our passing. Once we reached ground level, Gabby looked at me with concern.

"Scratch, do you have any idea what could have made that hole?"

"Not a one... and I don't want to be around when it shows

its face. C'mon, let's go find Bobby and round up Colin so we can get the hell out of here."

Some of the canine deaders had escaped the massacre, and I wanted to make sure we knew where they were headed. Gabby, Bobby, and I tracked them for a few miles at a distance, and as I suspected, they were headed northeast toward Austin. Confident that we could pick up their trail later, we headed back to the hospital for formal introductions with Bobby's Pack.

When we arrived, Colin and about a dozen of the Pack's members were gathered around a fire in the small patch of woods near the helipad. He was chatting with a Chuck Norris-looking guy wearing a leather biker vest, jeans, and boots. The guy was short and wiry, with a shaved head and an epic man beard. Despite the 'thrope's stature, I immediately pegged him for the Pack alpha by the way he carried himself.

Colin waved us over as we walked up. "Folks, there's someone I want you to meet. Scratch, meet Samson, former alpha of the Austin werewolf Pack, and now alpha of the Coastal Pack. Samson, meet Scratch..."

The alpha cut Colin off in a gruff, raspy voice. "I know who he is. So, you're the one who rescued my pup from those punters?"

"If you're referring to Bobby, I couldn't leave him with those assholes, so yes. And he's hardly a pup. He's pulled his weight and then some since then."

Samson glanced over at Bobby, who was conspicuously silent and avoiding eye contact with his adopted father. "I don't doubt it. Damn it, boy, but how you've grown."

Bobby merely acknowledged the attention with a shy smile, and Samson turned back to me.

"The boy always was headstrong, but we hadn't heard from him since he split." He looked at his adopted son. "Without permission, I might add."

Bobby's face darkened at that, so I decided to intervene before things got out of hand. Samson seemed like a stern leader, and given Bobby's personality I could easily see how they'd clash with each other.

"Does one of your Pack members always need permission to leave?" I asked. "I'm just curious, as I'm unfamiliar with your ways. In fact, the first time I saw a 'thrope was just a few weeks ago. Frankly, I'd like to learn more about you, and understand how your Pack differs from the wolves we ran into in Austin."

Samson ignored my question entirely. "Heard about that. Also heard you're responsible for taking them bastards out, including Van." He squinted at Colin with a smirk playing at the corners of his bearded mouth. "Colin's been known to pull lopsided victories out of his ass, but even he couldn't take out an entire werewolf pack... especially not one led by a primary. How'd you do it?"

I shrugged. "Teamwork, and a hell of a lot of luck. Plus, we had an alchemist and a golem."

Samson's eyes widened slightly. "Rabbi Borovitz? That wily old bastard still kicking around?"

Colin nodded. "Yeah, he is. He didn't recognize me, though. Of course, I only knew him by reputation."

Samson laughed. "The old man used to give those assholes at the Circle fits, that was for sure. They hated having rogue elements running loose, but Borovitz always had no fucks to give, especially where the Circle was concerned."

"What's 'The Circle'?" Gabby asked.

Samson glanced over at Gabby, as if noticing her for the first time. He sniffed the air in her direction, then gave Bobby a sideways glance. "Just some people who used to make life miserable for all the supernaturals in Austin... back before the War."

"What happened to them?" Gabby asked.

"They went underground, about the same time the fae went missing," Colin replied.

"And good riddance," a large and rather tough-looking member of the Pack interjected. "If one good thing came out of the apocalypse, it's that."

What Colin had said finally registered, and I held my hands up. "Hold up just a second... you can't just drop something like that in casual conversation and expect regular folk to let it slide. You mean *the* fae? As in, fairies and elves and crap?"

Colin nodded. "Told you, Scratch... there's a lot you don't know about the supernatural world. Zombies, vamps, and 'thropes are just touching the surface."

I sat down heavily on a stump someone had pulled up to the makeshift fire pit. "For the sake of discussion, let's just say that elves exist. Does someone want to explain how this all fits into our undead apocalypse?"

Colin and Samson looked at each other, but Samson was the first to speak up. "That's what I've been trying to figure out, ever since all this shit happened and the world went to hell. At first, we thought it was a coincidence—that the bombs fell, panic erupted, and then someone happened to get bit. Perfect storm for starting a zombie outbreak, what with the world in chaos and all.

"But then we heard it was happening all over, all at once. That's a bit too convenient to be a coincidence. So, me and what was left of my Pack started poking around all over the state. Austin, Houston, Dallas. Far as we can tell, the Dallas coven knows what caused it, and we think they're connected to whoever or whatever was behind it all." The alpha looked at

Colin. "I was hoping you'd be able to reveal a bit more of the mystery surrounding the whole mess."

Colin shrugged. "I'm as much in the dark as you. Hell, I spent the last eight years keeping a bunch of my friends alive, and keeping my head down. Living in the shadow of the Corridor Pack, I spent most of my time making sure they didn't come to eat my people in the middle of the night."

Samson nodded. "Smart, living right under the noses of the baddest predators on the block. I bet it helped keep the heat off you from the vamps and deaders. Still, I wish I would've known you were alive. Could've used your help down along the coast."

I cleared my throat. "This reminiscing and catching up is touching and all, but I still have a threat to deal with. So, if you don't mind, I'm going to gather up my people and track down those dogs, 'til they lead me to whoever is making the damned things."

Samson looked at Colin. "Necromancy?"

Colin frowned. "Looks that way."

The old alpha nodded as he regarded me. "I owe you a solid since you rescued my... Bobby. So, I'm going to leave him on loan to you, and I'm going to send a couple of my people with you to track these things back to their lair."

Not one to turn down help when it was offered, I nodded my assent. "Much obliged. After seeing how you dealt with those deader dogs, I'd be glad to have your people along."

"Deader dogs?" Samson asked.

"I keep calling them familiars, but the other name seems to have stuck," Colin replied.

The old wolf laughed. "I suppose it's as good a name as any. But take my advice—whatever made those things is packing some badass magical juju. Don't try taking them on by yourself. If you want to take them out, come back and let us help you."

"I'll consider it," was my only reply. "If you don't mind me asking, what are y'all going to do while we're gone?"

Samson gave Colin a look that spoke of plans within plans, and I got the feeling something had been decided before we'd arrived. "For now, we'll stick around here and run patrols around this 'Facility' of yours."

I frowned at Colin. "You told them about that?"

"You can trust them, Scratch. Samson and I go way back."

"Wasn't your decision to make, but it's too late now." I narrowed my eyes as I addressed Samson. "Nobody approaches the Facility until I get back. Last thing I need is a bunch of 'thropes to show up and freak everyone out. Things are tense enough as it is."

"It's your place, so it's your call," was all Samson said in reply.

I turned to give Colin a hard stare. "And as for you, when I get back we're going to have a long discussion about OPSEC."

"Whatever you say, Scratch."

He actually had the audacity to smile as he said it, and I found myself wishing I'd dislocated his knee back at the castle house.

———

We tracked the remains of the deader dog pack east and north over the course of two days without ever catching up to them. I was worried they'd head for Canyon Lake, but they skirted around it and made a beeline for Kyle, crossing IH-35—just south of the former bedroom community. From there, they continued in a north-northeasterly direction, moving quickly and never stopping in their efforts to get wherever the hell they were headed. They crossed 45 and 183, finally turning north as they led us through what were once sparsely-populated areas south of Austin.

The two 'thropes Samson had sent along with us were stoically silent during the entire trip. One was the big man who'd expressed his dislike of "The Circle," whatever the hell that was. He went by Sledge, and he looked like he'd earned the name. The other was a muscular Latina woman with short-cropped hair and a lot of ink. She said her name was Trina, and the permanent scowl on her face told me that was about all she was going to say.

To be honest, their reticence didn't bother me much at all. However, I noticed that they didn't act nearly as antisocial toward Bobby. In fact, they almost coddled him, for lack of a better term. Each of them spent a great deal of time watching him when he wasn't looking, which I interpreted as watching his back. It gave me the feeling that they weren't there so much to help us out as to make sure Bobby got back safely.

It also reminded me that there was a lot going on that I didn't understand, and I berated myself for sticking so close to the settlements all these years. I could've been getting out in the great wide world to make connections and gather intel on our enemy; if I had, I might not be in the dark so much now. But hell, hindsight's always 20/20, so I resolved to do my best to play catch up and learn all I could about the supernatural from here on out.

The dogs were well ahead of us by the time we realized where they were headed. Although Bobby and the other 'thropes could run forever, and Gabby would've if I'd let her, I found myself needing a bit more rest than usual. My bite was still acting up, and it pissed me off how much it slowed me down. I did my best to hide it, and we took a few breaks on our way to Austin in pursuit of the undead dogs that threatened our home.

Gabby and the 'thropes had taken turns following the trail, which led to a patch of woods along Onion Creek, just north of the old Travis County landfill and south of the airport. We arrived at night, taking cover to observe movement around the control tower in the distance. That was curious enough, but what really piqued my interest was all the activity at the old Armed Forces Reserve Center across the creek from us.

Sledge sniffed the air and scowled. "You smell that?" he asked Bobby and Trina.

Bobby nodded. "Vamps."

I belly-crawled up alongside them to get a better look. "Nos-types, or the higher variety?"

Trina's expression went from a scowl to a deep frown, and her worry lines deepened around her mouth and eyes. "The pretty kind, and lots of them. I don't like it. We're outnumbered and have no idea what they're up to. I say we do some quick recon and get the hell out of here."

I couldn't disagree with her, but I also needed to know what the hell a bunch of vamps were doing in Austin. We'd just only dealt with Piotr and his gang of 'thropes, and narrowly prevented an inter-dimensional vampire invasion from hell—or wherever the things originally came from. No way was I going to let these assholes try some crazy shit like that again.

I tapped Bobby on the shoulder to get his attention, as his eyes were glued on the Reserve Center. "Bobby, why don't you take Gabby and your packmates and hang back a bit? I'll stay here and keep an eye on the building, and once it gets light I'll take a closer look."

He shook his head and pursed his lips in a hard line. "I don't know, Scratch. I don't like it."

"I know, kiddo, but we didn't come all this way for nothing. I want answers, and I need to know the severity of the threat we're now facing. I'll wait for daylight and do a quick bit of recon, just like Trina said. Then, we'll haul ass back to the Facility and figure out our next move."

Bobby looked back at the buildings, where a half-dozen vamps were moving boxes and equipment onto an Army troop transport truck with superhuman speed. The rumbling clatter of a diesel engine firing up startled Gabby and got the gears inside my head turning.

"I'll be damned," I muttered. "Just where the hell do you think they're getting clean diesel from?"

Bobby pointedly ignored my question. "If you're going to take a closer look, just don't get caught, alright? I don't want to have to explain to Samson how I ended up in a fight with a bunch of vamps."

I smiled. "I'll be careful. Besides, how much trouble can I get into while these vamps are asleep?"

THE RESERVE CENTER consisted of five buildings: a large main office building with two wings, three large aircraft hangars by the helipads, and a motor pool building. I recalled that it had once served as the training center and headquarters for several Army and Marine reserve units, but I doubted there'd be any useful gear lying about. Scroungers and punters had probably been through the place a million times by now; what the vamps wanted here was a mystery to me.

But they'd obviously come looking for something, and I doubted it was military-grade weapons and gear. If I had to guess, there was intel stored here, locked up inside the place or hidden on some random computer's hard drive, and the vamps aimed to get it. Intel on what was a mystery, but whatever they were searching for, I intended to find out what it was and why they needed it.

The fact that they had working vehicles running on diesel fuel sure made me wonder what things were like in Dallas. I'd heard rumors that the vamps had revived certain industries and conveniences of modern living, but I'd taken it as nothing more than crazy talk. Not many people had made it in and out of

Dallas alive, so any news that came out of there was always taken as two parts hearsay and one part speculation. But before daybreak, I'd seen half a dozen vamps flitting around, loading boxes and computer equipment into that transport truck and a couple of Humvees.

So, I had to accept that somewhere, someone had gotten a refinery working again—and perhaps the vamps even had a few oil wells running as well. Lord knew there were tons of them scattered across the state, so it wouldn't be a stretch to think they'd gotten a few producing crude again.

But enough with speculating about which technologies the vamps had revived. I needed to find out what the hell they were up to inside that building. I waited for first light, then began sneaking my way closer to the grounds.

Doing so wasn't hard, as there was plenty of cover between the creek and the Reserve Center. Deaders were scarce in the area, and I was able to steer clear of the few stragglers milling about as I made my way to the military installation. I was completely exposed when I crossed Burleson Road, but after that, all the overgrowth kept me hidden as I approached from the southwest. I entered the facility by walking over a section of downed chain link fence, then crept through the undergrowth toward the south hangar.

A quick peek through a window in one of the hangar entrances revealed there was nothing of interest inside for the vamps. By all appearances, the place had been untouched. However, dead bodies scattered all over the grounds and inside the building revealed that a pitched battle had taken place here —probably in the early days of the invasion. From the looks of it, it hadn't gone well for the soldiers and Marines. The corpses told a tale of checkpoints and cordons that had been overrun.

I left the dead to their silent rest, and continued on toward the main building. That was where I'd seen most of the activity, so I assumed it would also be where the vamps' plans would be revealed. I decided to start with the transport truck, to see what the hell they were collecting.

Stooping to maintain a low profile, I ran through the weeds and brush toward my goal. Halfway there, I vaulted an interior fence to access the parking area behind the main building, then I crouched in the tall weeds and overgrowth to assess the situation. Feeling eyes upon me, I searched the area for the culprit, or culprits.

There. Two deader dogs had rounded the corner of the building, and they were now looking my direction. I reached back and adjusted the sword scabbard across my back, then drew my katana as quietly and with as little movement as possible. The reflection of sunlight on the blade betrayed my presence, and the hounds began loping silently across the concrete lot toward me.

The undead abominations closed in on me fast. A flash of steel decapitated the lead dog, and a backhanded slash with a sidestep took out the second as it leapt for my throat. I nudged the bodies with my toe to make sure they were down for the count, then continued on, sword in hand.

Skirting the exterior of the main building, I made it around to the front, using burned out military vehicles and crumbling sandbag walls for cover as I crossed the lot to the parked transport truck. Checking the building to ensure I wasn't being observed, I climbed into the back of the truck to see what they'd been loading up.

Inside were stacks of filing boxes, along with about a dozen computers and laptops sans monitors. With no way to fire up the computers, I began digging through the boxes. Each was loaded to the top with file after file, most of which were memos and reports on troop readiness and whatnot. It was typical military brass bullshit; every minute of an officer's existence in a command unit was spent justifying their next promotion with reports and stats. I rifled through box after box, until something caught my eye.

I came across several files that were labeled "Pantex." *What the actual hell?*

Looking through the folders, I soon realized exactly what the vamps were up to. Pantex was a facility outside of Amarillo that few people knew about. Its existence wasn't top secret, but it was a sort of open secret that the U.S. government and military hadn't made a big deal of before the War. The Pantex facility had once been operated by the Department of Energy and a private company called Consolidated Nuclear Security, LLC.

I only knew about it because it was one of those places where a lot of high speed ex-military guys got cushy security jobs after they got out. A person might wonder why the Department of Energy and a private company would need to hire a bunch of ex-special ops soldiers to run security for their facility. They hired top-tier operators so they'd have the very best guarding the place, because Pantex existed for one purpose, and one purpose only.

That purpose was the dismantling of nuclear weapons and the long-term storage of weapons-grade plutonium. And if I had to take a stab at what the vamps were up to, I'd say they wanted to get their hands on all the plutonium that was in deep storage at Pantex, in order to blow another hole between our world and theirs.

The thing was, I needed to know for sure. And, that meant I needed more intel—human intel—in order to verify my suspicions. Since there weren't any humans around, I'd have to do with the next best thing. Meaning, I intended to sneak inside that building to abduct a vampire while it rested in deep, blissful sleep.

Now, I didn't really know the first thing about the physiology and sleep habits of higher vamps. But I had staked more than my share of nosferatu over the years, and many times I'd done it while they were sleeping. Nos-types went into an almost coma-like state during the day. And when they did, they were vulnerable.

In the past, when I happened across a vamp getting their beauty rest, I'd usually shoot them, stake them, or behead them —depending on my mood and what gear I had on me. But for this particular crazy scheme, I'd need to successfully capture and abduct a vamp within its lair, and then transport it away in broad daylight without killing the damned thing. I figured that once I got it back to the Pack, they'd help me torture and interrogate the thing, and that's how we'd get our intel.

Or so I assumed. For all I knew, the 'thropes were just as clueless about higher vamps as I was. I doubted it, but it was possible. If that happened to be the case, I'd improvise. There had to be a way to get one of them to talk. If there was, I'd find it.

But first, I had to abduct one of the damned things. Which meant sneaking into the building, which was probably being guarded by the remainder of the deader dogs we'd chased there. Oh, and I couldn't forget the witch—because she was probably in there, too.

Alright, no sweat. I can do this, I thought to myself as I snuck my way over to the front doors of the Reserve Center. I doubted that any of the vamps would be on watch now that the sun was up, but there were at least four more deader dogs running about. I had a feeling they'd be guarding the vamps while they slept, and possibly patrolling the halls inside the place. I'd need to be on my toes.

Katana in hand, I pulled on the glass entrance door. *Locked. You have got to be freaking kidding me.* I tried the others, all locked. *Shit.*

I backed up and looked around for a broken window, or some other means to get inside the place. After 9/11, all federal buildings had been built with blast-proof glass that was resistant to hurricane-force winds and, in some cases, small caliber rounds. Even though downtown Austin had taken a small nuclear missile right in the teeth at ground level when the bombs dropped, most of these windows were still intact. And the ones that weren't were all on the upper floors.

Shit, shit, shit. I walked the perimeter of the place, trying access doors and fire exits, but all were locked. Surely there had to be another way in, via roof access or something. I walked around the building again, looking for some means of ingress. *There.*

Up on the third story, there was a window that looked like it'd been hit by large-caliber machine gunfire. It'd probably happened back when they were fighting off the initial swarm of deaders. The holes in the glass meant the window pane had been weakened, so chances were good I could kick it in... and hopefully not bring the rest of those deader dogs running.

I shimmied up a drain pipe to get on the second-floor roof, and that gave me access to the third-floor windows. A few well-placed kicks, and I was inside the building, in some sort of conference room or classroom. I waited for a minute or more, listening for any sign that I'd drawn unwanted attention, but it appeared I was in the clear. For now, anyway.

Blade in hand, I crept to the door and began exploring the place.

The Reserve Center building I was in was massive, three floors tall with two large wings housing offices, logistics centers, training rooms and classrooms, a mess hall, fitness facilities, and more. I spent at least an hour checking every room on every floor, but there was no sign of the vamps or their four-legged companions. Since there were windows in most of the rooms, there was also plenty of sunlight in the place. So, if there were vamps here, they'd have to be in a sublevel somewhere, hiding out from all these UV rays.

That meant I was going underground.

I found a doorway to a stairwell that led below ground level. The door had been left closed, but unlocked. Apparently, the vamps felt comfortable with their safety in these parts. If they were anything like Piotr was, it was hard to blame them for being cocky. That vamp had moved like a mongoose on speed, and he was strong as an ox. Besides that, few humans came through these parts outside of the odd punter gang or a scav crew... and they'd just be an easy meal for these bloodsuckers.

A glance inside the stairwell showed me it was almost completely void of light. My enhanced vision was good, but not that good, so I'd need some sort of secondary source of light— one that wouldn't give me away to anything creeping around down there. I dug around inside my bag for my self-powered LED flashlight and spent a couple of minutes charging it with the crank. The noise sounded deafening in the silence of the building, but I'd already checked the floors above-ground and knew they were clear of enemies. Once the light was charged, I taped a red lens from a milspec flashlight I'd found over the lens of the LED flashlight.

Voila, instant tactical flashlight.

As any infantryman knew, red light was harder to see at a

distance in the dark than white light. So, by taping the red lens over my light, I'd draw less attention to myself below—but I'd still have plenty of light to see by, at least as long as the charge lasted. It wouldn't last long, so I'd have to be quick.

I headed down the stairs, into the sublevel of the Reserve Center. This was likely where the armory had been located, as well as where they would have stored sensitive documents and other restricted information. I exited the stairwell into a nondescript hallway that was littered with dead bodies, ones that had been there for years. Some had come to a violent end at the hands of deaders, while others had died of self-inflicted wounds.

I ignored the story the life-sized diorama told, because I'd seen it too many times over the last eight years to be distracted by such sights. Puzzling out exactly what had happened was a moot point, because it wasn't going to bring the dead back to life. Instead, I was more concerned with what might be *un*dead down here. I stood still as a statue by the stairway exit, listening for the now familiar *click-click-click* of canine claws on tile.

Nothing.

As silent as the damned things were, I might stumble on them at any moment, keeping watch while their masters slept. That gave me pause, but I really wanted the intel that abducting one of these vamps might provide. I tightened my grip on my sword and trudged on down the hall, heart beating a steady cadence in my chest that betrayed the rush of adrenaline I felt. I stopped at each door I came to, listening for any sound or sign of movement before I looked inside.

Most of the doors were open, blocked by bodies or debris from the battle that had taken out the last survivors at this facility. I swept the floor, room by room. *Empty. Empty. Empty.* They were all empty, and I was just about to reconsider whether the vamps were here at all, when I opened an office door and my light swept across a familiar and heartbreaking sight.

Kara? She was lying on top of a desk, statuesque and as lovely as ever in repose. Her face was perfect, and more beautiful than I remembered. But she remained corpse-like and silent, perfectly still in the eerie rest that the undead required during daylight hours.

I tiptoed up to her, shining the light so I could clearly see her face, to make certain it was her. It was. My heart skipped a beat before it broke a little more, seeing her lying before me, exquisitely preserved in this preternatural state of undeath. She was more than perfect, actually. Vampirism had taken what beauty nature had given her and magnified it tenfold. I wondered if that was a side effect of the vyrus, and decided she must've been newly turned when I'd attempted to rescue her from Piotr and the Corridor Pack, back at the research campus.

I reached out to stroke her face, then paused, afraid that my touch would prove this all to be an illusion. Instead, I leaned over her, whispering in the lowest voice I could muster.

"Kara—"

Her eyes snapped open, and her face transformed before my eyes. I stumbled backward, tripping over a file box and falling hard until my head and back hit the wall. Still, I never took my eyes off the creature before me as her features shifted and reformed into that of a stranger.

Kara's freckled, wind-chafed skin blurred, to be replaced by a porcelain-perfect face—unmarred by blemish and completely devoid of color, save a slight blush around the cheeks. This woman's hair and eyes darkened; her lips became fuller and redder. As she metamorphosed, the change revealed high cheekbones and a large nose that dominated her face without detracting from her beauty. She was barefoot, and wore a slinky, low-cut black dress that revealed long, shapely legs and a dancer's chest. The dress was something that would've been expensive before the War, an anachronism no human would bother with in the post-war world of violence and survival.

"That's a cruel trick," I stated, catching my balance as I took a defensive stance with my sword held in front of me.

I briefly considered going on the attack, but held back. This creature had seen Kara, that much was certain, else she wouldn't have been able to fool me so completely. And while I was unsure whether I'd witnessed some sort of mental trick, an actual physical transformation, or an honest-to-goodness magical illusion, I didn't care at the moment. This *thing* knew something about Kara's whereabouts, and I was going to find out what.

She sat up and swung her legs off the desk, crossing them as she regarded me with a cruel smile. "It is, and one I couldn't help but play on you. I've had my pets searching for you—and your lover—since my brother's death. He cried out to me through the bond we shared, at the moment of his death." Her voice was peculiarly accented, something Eastern European that I couldn't place.

"He had it coming," I said, keeping my eyes on her.

"He had nothing coming but the right to rule all humans as the miserable cattle you are!" she hissed, showing her fangs before she composed herself in an unsettling and instant change in demeanor. "When he died, I experienced it through our bond. I felt you stab him in the back with that poisoned blade, and saw his spawn betray him as she snapped his neck. You know of whom I speak. You've put yourself through hell trying to rescue her, after all. The same way I'd have sacrificed myself to save my beloved Piotr."

"Where's Kara?" I snarled.

"To be honest, I have no idea—although not for lack of searching. She's proven to be... most elusive, for a new vampire. Of course, Piotr was very old, and very powerful, and without doubt he conferred some of that power on your love when he turned her. So, it's no surprise that she's managed to evade me thus far."

"If you hurt her, I'll—"

My words were cut off by the vamp's iron grip on my throat. She'd covered the distance between us in the blink of an eye, batting the sword from my grasp and pinning me to the wall with one hand around my throat. My feet dangled as I kicked, helplessly, clawing at her arm with little effect. She squeezed tighter, cutting off the blood to my brain, until my vision began to dim. I blacked out, and when I came back around I was sitting on the floor, back to the wall with the vamp squatting next to me.

"You'll do nothing, hunter. I've killed dozens like you over the centuries. Each thought they were worthy. Some even dabbled in the mystical arts, or traded pieces of their soul to things darker than I, in futile attempts to gain some edge that would allow them to prove victorious against me. None survived."

"If you hurt Kara, I will kill you," I growled.

In a flash of movement, she grabbed my sword where it had fallen, stabbing it through my shoulder and pinning me to the wall. I screamed in rage and pain, grasping the handle of the weapon in an attempt to pull it free so I could thrust it in her heart. It wouldn't budge. Blood dripped around the wound, creating a slowly spreading stain as it leaked down my chest.

She leaned in and sniffed the air close to my face, and her expression soured. "I can smell the sickness in you, the stink of rot and death. Your body fights against it, but despite what small advantages medical science has granted you, eventually you will succumb."

She caressed my face, almost tenderly. I attempted to bat her hand away, but I may as well have been slapping an iron bar. She let her hand fall, and I did the same, weakening from blood loss and shock.

"What do you creatures want?" I asked.

She played with a lock of my hair, and I batted at her hand to little effect. "To rule, of course. To dominate. To bring humanity to its knees."

"Obviously—but none of it makes sense. Why kill the thing that sustains you? Why wipe out your only source of food on the planet?"

She chuckled, a low rumble in her throat that stood in sharp contrast to the high, almost soothing tone of her voice. "Do you really think we'd kill you all off, and doom ourselves to starvation? We'd been breeding you like cattle, long before we dropped the bombs and unleashed the undead against you. Honestly, how many of you do you think we require to survive?

"You humans had spread like an infection all across the

world, a disease that threatened to destroy itself by killing its host. You were a greater threat to your own survival than we ever were! We saw our own destruction inevitably entwined with your own, so we had to act to ensure the future of our people."

"You're telling me this was all about eugenics and environmentalism? About population control and saving the earth?"

The vampire shook her head. "You act as though you're unaware of the path down which your species was headed. Have you so soon forgotten the way the world was before we intervened? The seas were filled with garbage and debris. Radiation and toxins had poisoned the oceans. Coral reefs were dying all over the globe, along with the entire ecosystems they supported. Ten thousand animal species were driven to extinction each year. Global surface temperatures were rising, the polar ice caps were melting, and yet your species refused to recognize the signs. We had no choice but to act."

I laughed, despite the intense pain and nausea I felt.

The vamp's eyes narrowed. "What about all I've said do you find so amusing?"

I waved a hand dismissively at her. "Oh, it's not that. I'm laughing because it's just my luck that I run into a vampire who's also a tree-hugging environmentalist."

I never saw the blow, but I heard the crack as her hand struck my cheek, and felt the whiplash effect of my head snapping around before I faded out. However long it took me to come back around, I had no idea, but she was still squatting there in front of me when I regained consciousness.

"This is no laughing matter, human. We've lived on this planet side by side with you for millennia, since the dawn of history. Your world is a paradise compared to our own, and those of other supernatural entities who've come here. Why do you think they clamor and fight to reach your world? I'll tell you why. It's because hell truly exists, just on the other side of the Veil.

"And now it exists here as well... for your kind, anyway. But for my kind, we've never had it better. We breed humans for food, we enjoy all the creature comforts human technology can provide, and we rule this world as royalty, as is our due. With better than ninety percent of your population culled, there still exist plenty of your kind to enslave, hunt, and feed on as we see fit. And as this planet recovers from the relatively minor insult we visited on it, the future is looking very, very bright for my kind... and quite bleak for your own."

I was starting to fade out, maybe from blood loss or a concussion. I'd only just recovered from my fight with Piotr, and I doubted the slap she'd given me had done my brain any good. Still, I struggled to remain conscious, because I wanted answers.

"You're trying to bring more of your kind over here, aren't you? But why not just make more of yourselves?"

She rocked back on her heels, then up on her toes, perching like a bird of prey. "Because our offspring don't always share our values, as your Kara has shown. Often, they fight against us, rebelling like the children they are. But when the master brings the remainder of our kind over here, we'll be unstoppable. Then, no force or species on this earth will be able to stand against Marduk and his people."

"You should kill me now," I whispered. "I'll kill you, and this Marduk. You can count on it."

She sneered, licking her lips and playing the tip of her tongue across one of her oversized canines. "How I wish you were healthy so I might feed off you, just so you could feel what it is to be utterly and completely dominated. But I'm afraid the act might kill you, and I intend to keep you alive so your lover can watch you die a slow, painful death."

She stood, leaning over me to grab the sword's handle,

twisting it as she spoke. "When you see your lover—and I know you will—tell her that Calypso comes for her."

She released her grip on the sword and strutted out of the room, slowly, at human speed. I watched her go, then blacked out.

I woke on a field stretcher, inside some sort of warehouse or repair shop. I had an I.V. tube and needle in my arm, and there was a bag of saline hung on the wall nearby. I was covered in wool military blankets, and I had a splitting headache. Someone had patched up my shoulder; apparently, Calypso hadn't hit anything vital. I imagined that was by design.

However, the whole side of my face where she'd slapped was swollen. I tongued my teeth and found a loose molar. Hopefully, it'd heal back in place if I left it alone. Dental care was hard to get these days.

I watched the steady *drip, drip, drip* of saline solution fall inside the I.V. drip chamber as I got a handle on my surroundings. I heard voices nearby—Bobby, Gabby, and the 'thropes, along with the crackle of a fire. I tried to sit up, but dizziness and weakness dictated otherwise. On top of it all, my bite ached like a son of a bitch.

"Hey, it wakes!" Bobby said from nearby. He closed the distance and took a knee beside the cot. "You're lucky that Trina used to be an EMT before the War."

"Paramedic!" she exclaimed from nearby, with exasperation in her voice. "There's a difference."

Bobby stuck his finger in the air and spun it in circles. "Fine, paramedic. Anyway, when you didn't come back we went looking for you. Someone left a note, saying you were in the basement. We found you downstairs, bleeding and unconscious with your sword stuck through your shoulder."

"Where are the vamps?"

Gabby stood at the foot of the cot, tapping her toe and giving me the evil eye. "Long gone, by the time we got there, along with the rest of the deader dogs. Although we did find the ones you killed." She exhaled sharply and crossed her arms. "You could have died, *cabrón*. What is it with you and this death wish you have?"

"Nice to see you too, Gabby." I sighed, and the effort made my head throb. "I assure you, I don't have a death wish. I looked around outside the place, and once I figured out what they were looking for, I figured we'd want more info."

Trina walked over and nudged Bobby out of the way. She checked my pulse and looked at my stab wound as she spoke. "So you went inside a vamp's lair by yourself? That's dumb, even by Bobby's standards."

"Hey!" he protested.

I shook my head slightly. "How was I supposed to know one of them would be awake?"

She finished checking my bandage, replacing my clothing and blankets before she stood. "Damn, must've been an older one. That's shitty luck. They don't need as much rest as the young ones. And the really old, powerful ones don't sleep at all. You're lucky you made it out of there alive."

I nodded and coughed, wishing I hadn't. Every time I moved, I hurt. "The more you know, right? Anyway, she said she wants me alive. Apparently, she intends to exact some kind of revenge on me and Kara."

Sledge spoke from over by the fire. "Who's Kara?"

"His ex," Gabby said. She turned and looked at me. "But Kara's long gone, right? I mean, how's this vamp going to hatch this plan of hers when your girlfriend has skipped town?"

"Okay, first off, she's not my 'ex' anything. And second—"

"Duh, Scratch, she's a vamp," Gabby said with an eye roll and all the sarcasm a teenage voice could muster. "I hate to tell you this, but you two have some compatibility issues."

Trina's jaw dropped. "Your ex is a vamp? Never been with a vamp before. Ain't that kind of like sleeping with a corpse?"

"She was human until recently," Bobby said. "She got turned before we could rescue her from Piotr."

I nodded with a wince. "Who happens to be this Calypso's brother, or so she says. Since Kara and I killed him, now she's out for vengeance."

"Great," Gabby muttered.

"Oh, it gets worse. When I looked through the files they were pulling from the building, I found several documents referencing the old Pantex facility up near Amarillo."

Trina whistled. "Nuclear shit. Man, that's bad news. Back before the War, I used to go to EMS conferences, and that was one of the facilities that gave the counter-terror people nightmares. We used to run scenarios about what would happen if it was ever attacked."

"I don't get it," Bobby said.

I raised my hand to get his attention. "Then let me make it clear. Before the War, that place was where the government disassembled and stored any nuclear weapons that were being put out of commission. It's probably full of weapons-grade plutonium. Remember that portal thing Piotr was working on?"

"How could I forget?" Bobby said. "I still have nightmares about it."

"Yeah, well, chew on this. I think once the vamps have their hands on a load of plutonium, they're going try to punch another hole in reality, to bring the rest of their kind over from the other side."

Trina wanted to wait another day before they moved me, to allow me to heal up a bit more to avoid reopening the wound. But I insisted we couldn't wait. I sent Bobby on ahead to warn the others, and Sledge and Trina carried me on the stretcher as we headed back to the Facility.

By the second day I was able to walk, but they ended up carrying me anyway, since we'd made quicker time that way. Gabby scouted ahead, and cleared the path of deaders where she could. When she couldn't, she gave fair warning and steered us around any sizable groups that were in our way. Bobby rejoined us that evening, and we made it back by the morning of the third day.

True to his word, Samson had his Pack members running patrols around the Facility while we were gone. Colin had told everyone they were on lockdown until we got the deader dog situation under control, which more or less kept anyone from getting a peek outside. I hated to think what would happen if one of the abductees sighted one of Samson's werewolves; it'd cause outright pandemonium.

Once we got back, I had Colin bring Anna and Mickey outside to one of the old training buildings on base, so we could have a pow-wow and figure out our next move. When we were all gathered, I started the meeting and got down to business.

"First things first. Did you have any trouble from those hounds while we were gone?"

Samson shook his head. "We spotted one or two here and there, but whenever we tried to engage them they'd take off. I got the feeling they were running surveillance on us. We managed to kill a few, but some of them got away."

Colin nodded. "It's Calypso. She's keeping an eye on us. If she's the one running them, that is."

"I told you what I saw," I said, looking Colin in the eye. "I don't know if it was magic or some sort of mind trick, but she looked just like Kara. Then, she changed right before my eyes. The only thing I can compare it to is like when a 'thrope shifts."

The big swordsman stroked his chin. "It sounds like illusory magic to me. And if she's the one who created those familiars, this is bad—real bad. A powerful witch is trouble enough. But a vampire who is also a witch? And one who dabbles in necromancy? She's going to be hell to stop, believe me."

Anna tapped a finger on the map we had laid out on the table in front of us. "You say that facility is in Amarillo? What are the chances they're already trying to get in?"

I shook my head. "No idea. But, something tells me that the intel Calypso came for is the key to getting inside that facility. I'm sure they had failsafes in place before the War, to lock the place down in case of a total power failure. No way they're getting in without powering the place up again and having the codes to get inside."

"Unless they used high explosives," Sledge interjected.

I shook my head. "That's a possibility, but I think they'd have already done that if they thought it would work. No, they're waiting for that intel. That's the key."

Mickey cleared his throat. "You think they headed back with it already?"

"Not likely." I ran my finger from the former capital to Dallas, along IH-35. "It's a hell of a long way from Austin to Dallas, along roads that are choked with wrecked and ruined vehicles and other debris. Not to mention looters, punters, scavs, and deaders. Plus, they have to hide during the daytime. No, I think it took them a while to get down here, and I don't think Calypso is going to take a jaunt back until she finishes her business—all of it."

"Meaning you and Kara," Anna said.

"Exactly," I replied. "She has a real hard on for both of us, and I think she wants to punish us in some way, in order to get revenge for Piotr's death. So, she'll stay down here until she knows we're within her grasp."

"Then what?" Bobby asked.

"Then she'll bring hell down on us all," Colin said. "Based on what you reported, she's traveling with a half-dozen higher vamps. The bad news? Even a handful of older vamps are more than a match for Samson's Pack"—he paused to glance at Samson—"no offense, of course."

Samson gave a slight nod. "None taken. If these vamps are young, second or third-gen bloodsuckers, I give my people even odds against any of them. But if they're older? We'd need three-to-one odds to even stand a chance."

Colin closed his eyes and knuckled his forehead. "Add to that any familiars she has in reserve, her potential ability to command the undead, and whatever other magical powers she possesses... I don't know, Scratch. I'm just not sure we can beat her, at least not without suffering serious casualties."

A high, nasally woman's voice cut in as the door to the building opened. "Then why are we even planning to fight these vampires in the first place? Why aren't we negotiating with them instead?"

I let out a short sigh of exasperation. "Nadine. How kind of you to crash our party."

She stormed into the center of the room, eyeing me with the kind of contempt normally reserved for IRS agents and debt collectors. "And it's just like you to leave out the common folk, Scratch. As if you and your weirdo friends are too good for us."

"It's not that, Nadine. I just didn't want to start a panic."

"Too late for that!" she screeched. "You've got those poor people all in an uproar, what with your secret meetings and consorting with these... inhuman creatures." She spat on the floor for emphasis. "And, like always, you're the one who's the cause of all our troubles. I say we just hand you and your girlfriend over, and save ourselves the trouble of dying at the hands of these vampires. They can go back to Dallas with you two, and leave us alone like they have been."

And that's when our meeting erupted into chaos.

FATAL

NADINE WAS BECOMING QUITE the liability. As it turned out, she'd been secretly eavesdropping on our conversations for some time. How she'd managed it, I had no idea—but apparently the bitch had been filling the settlers' heads with all sorts of nonsense. I needed to do something about her, and fast, before she turned out to be the death of us all.

After the meeting-slash-screaming-session was over, I headed back inside the Facility to find the Doc so I could fill her in; or, at least, that was my intention. I never found her, because a sea of people immediately surrounded me the minute I set foot inside. Folks asked me all manner of questions that I simply didn't have answers for—or didn't care to answer.

"Is it true you're secretly conspiring with 'thropes?"

"Have you been infected?"

"Are those zombie dogs going to eat us all?"

"Nadine says you're going to kick us out and leave us to the vamps. Is that true?"

And on, and on. Finally, I'd had enough. I drew my sidearm and fired it into the ceiling. That got their attention.

"Everyone just calm the hell down! We're not 'conspiring'

with anyone. You all know Bobby is a 'thrope, and that he helped rescue you. His Pack is now helping protect this facility —from the so-called 'zombie dogs,' I might add. No one is kicking anyone out, but I just might if you people don't settle down and get with the program!

"I suggest that you figure out if you prefer living in a secure, underground facility with electricity, clean running water, and no deaders for miles around. Because if so, then I expect you all to stop squabbling, pitch in, and do what the hell you're told. Otherwise, you're dead weight—and frankly, I don't have time to babysit a bunch of whiny-ass people while I'm trying to save them from hell on earth."

Some two dozen sets of eyes stared at me as if I were mad... and I supposed I was. I realized I was waving my pistol around, and re-holstered it before I was tempted to accidentally shoot someone on purpose.

"Now, go about your business, and tomorrow I'll start assigning job duties and work rosters, to ensure that everyone has a job to do and work to keep them out of trouble." They continued looking at me, some with shock written on their faces, and others with defiance in their eyes. "Did I stutter? Dismissed!"

As the crowd dispersed with a great deal of mumbling and grumbling, I heard the Doc's voice behind me. "Treating a group of civilians like they're in the military is probably not the best way to gain their trust and support."

I turned around to find her lurking in a nearby doorway, conveniently out of sight. "Nice of you to show your face, Captain Perez. Perhaps if you'd done as I asked and maintained some semblance of order around here, I wouldn't have to."

She tsked. "For one, I'm too busy trying to come up with a vaccine that'll save you and all of them to be bothered with these petty spats and concerns. And second, it was your idea to bring these people here. What exactly did you expect would happen? Did you think they'd be appreciative? That they'd help you build a utopia and it'd all be unicorns and rainbows from here on out? Because if you did, I have news for you—that's just not how people work."

I sighed and rubbed my shoulder. It was healing, but it hurt almost as bad as my deader bite. "Sorry to snap at you. I'm just tired and fed up, is all."

She tilted her head and gave me a grim, concerned smile. "I suppose I can give you a pass this time, considering how you were recently skewered by a vamp and all."

"You heard, huh?"

"The chachalaca and my adopted niece filled me in, almost as soon as they got back. Gabby is some kind of upset with you, for putting yourself at risk again."

"She's a teenager. When is she not upset? Anyway, we have bigger concerns." I glanced around to make sure no one was looking, and pulled up my sleeve. "It's getting worse."

The Doc looked at the site of my deader bite and hissed. "Scratch, you should have said something. The infection has spread again. The venom has progressed at least five centimeters since the last time I looked at it."

I pushed the sleeve back down and clucked my tongue. "I was a little preoccupied, what with making it back from Austin in one piece and the deader dog problem."

She grabbed my arm and exposed the bite again, turning it this way and that as she examined it more closely. "Yes, well... I may have something that can help that. Not a cure, mind you, but something to help fight off the infection. I've been working furiously with the last blood sample I took from you, and I think I might have made a breakthrough."

"A vaccine?" She blinked her eyes, then nodded once. I whistled softly. "How soon before you think it'll be ready?"

"That depends on how well my guinea pig responds to it."

I tried to laugh, but it turned into a cough that made my shoulder and head ache in equal measures. "Your guinea pig is falling apart as we speak. Whatever it does to me, it can't possibly make things worse."

"Famous last words," she said, sucking on her lower lip as she regarded me gravely. "Meet me down in the lab in thirty, and we'll find out."

"Will do. And while we're at it, I'll fill you in on everything that happened on our little excursion to Austin. I've got a bad feeling about this, Doc."

"How so? We've dealt with bad situations before, Scratch."

"Yeah, but not like this. Somehow, I think our troubles are just beginning."

Downstairs in the lab, the Doc gave me several injections that stung like the dickens and made me woozy. "What the hell is in there, Doc?"

She hooked me up to an EKG machine, a blood pressure cuff, and a pulse oximeter to monitor my vital signs. "It's a toxoid vaccine. It won't kill the deader vyrus, but it will help your body build up an immunity to its effects."

"How's it work... or do I even want to know?"

"Up until now, your body has been attempting to 'wall off' the deader venom. It's been an effective stop-gap measure, but only that. This should get your entire immune system to kick in and create antibodies against the toxin created by the deader virus. The vyrus infects by first killing live cells, then it enters them and takes over, reanimating the cell. Cell death is a prerequisite to zombification—the gangrenous lines you see emanating from your bite scar are evidence of that process. This vaccine will boost your immune system as it prevents that from spreading, and perhaps even allow your body to eradicate it over time."

My head began spinning, so I laid my head back on the gurney. "So, people who get this vaccine won't turn into zombies if they get bit, but they'll still be infected."

"That's exactly right; they'll still be carriers. They'll need to take precautions around anyone who hasn't received the vaccine."

I closed my eyes, waiting for a wave of nausea to pass. "Still, it's something to give people hope..."

My words were cut off by klaxons sounding and spinning lights flashing in the lab. I sat up and nearly fell off the gurney due to the effects of the vaccine. "Doc, what the hell is that?"

She jumped in front of a computer monitor and keyboard and typed in a few short commands. "Damn it—it's the sensors on the upper level. We have undead inside the Facility."

"Crap." I tore off the monitoring cables and blood pressure cuff as I swung my legs off the side of the gurney. My head was still spinning, but I'd fought battles in worse shape. "Help me get to my gear."

The Doc reached into a nearby drawer and grabbed a Beretta nine-millimeter pistol and two spare magazines. She tucked the mags into a pocket of her lab coat, then ducked under my arm and helped me over to where I'd left my gear. I strapped on my belt and holster and slung my rifle's one-point sling over my head, checking the mag and chambering a round.

The Doc led me to the exit. She helped me up the stairs, and we leaned against the wall on either side of the door to the upper level.

"You ready?" I asked, rifle at the ready.

"As I'll ever be." She typed in a code on the keypad and the door slid open. "The system will lock anyone out who doesn't have that code. If something happens to me, Gabby knows it."

I stumbled through the doorway, but the Doc stopped me with a hand on my shoulder. "Scratch, if it's as bad as I think it is, you may see a side of me you haven't seen before."

"I know you can take care of yourself, Lorena. Just watch your ass, alright?"

"I... sure, Scratch. Now go. I'll cover you."

I weaved my way into the hall and around a corner as the door whooshed closed behind us. Inside the halls of the upper level, it was chaos. Gunfire, cries of pain, and screams of terror echoed from every side, along with the moans of the dead and snarls that I hoped were coming from Bobby and the Pack. Bodies were strewn here and there, ripped open by claws or teeth, and the floor was slick with blood wherever our people had fallen.

I staggered toward the mess hall, using the wall to support myself. That was where I suspected the survivors would be making a stand, as most of the gunfire was coming from that direction. I looked back to check on the Doc, but she was gone; I'd just have to trust that she was capable of taking care of herself.

I turned another corner and found three of those damned deader dogs tearing a human body apart. I shot each in the head, then drew my sword to finish the job. Adrenaline was doing its work now, and though I still felt dizzy, it wasn't as severe. I tried to avoid looking at the body, compartmentalizing the casualties for now. I'd have time to sort that out later, but for now they were just corpses to me.

Something blurred into the hallway ahead of me—a short, wiry Caucasian man with slicked back red hair and a goatee. He wore khaki BDU pants, a black long-sleeved rash guard, and desert combat boots. His hands and mouth were covered in fresh blood and bits of gore, and blood flecked his face here and there in stark contrast to his pale, freckled skin.

"Well, fancy seeing you here, mate. The boss said you'd be here, but unfortunately you're a bit late to the party." He spoke with an Australian accent, which told me he probably wasn't that old. The accent hadn't fully developed on the continent until the mid-1800s, which meant this bloodsucker wasn't likely to be as ancient as Piotr or Calypso.

That meant I might have a chance.

I drew my sidearm and charged the vamp, running with my sword in my left hand. He wasn't nearly as quick as his boss, and I was loaded with silver-tipped hollow points. So, when my bullets punched three neat holes in his chest and torso, they had an effect. The vamp staggered, looking down at his chest.

"Well, that's hardly sporting, innit?" he said, then lunged at me, faster than any human or 'thrope could move.

I'd expected it. From what I'd seen, these higher vamps had little sophistication in their method of combat, and they relied on brute strength and speed over finesse and skill. While this asshole could move like Agent Smith, I didn't need to beat him to the punch.

All I needed to do was be in the right place when he moved.

One side effect of the Doc's serum that hadn't failed me yet was an increased perception speed. Although my body hadn't sped up much, my brain seemed to process visual inputs much, much faster. That allowed me to react to what my opponents were doing almost as soon as they moved. The vamp had a good dozen feet to cover, and while he was doing that I dropped the pistol, crouched, and swung at knee level with my sword.

My blade severed his right leg neatly, just below the knee. It was good, traditionally-forged Japanese steel, and I kept it razor sharp. The stroke combined with the vamp's forward momentum meant that I felt little resistance while the katana passed through the vamp's leg, even when it severed bone.

He tumbled over me in a heap, catching me on the shoulder with a swipe of his claws as he passed. I felt them cut deep, but adrenaline and anger allowed me to ignore the pain. I grabbed my pistol and spun, firing a single round into his skull before he could recover. Then, I walked up to him, weaving just slightly, and chopped his head off.

The pistol and sword combination seemed to be working for me, so I switched the katana to my strong side and held the pistol in my left hand as I entered the mess hall. By the time I arrived, the battle was already over. Several fully-transformed werewolves were standing in a circle around a small group of six or seven humans. There were dead bodies everywhere; I assumed the single decapitated corpse had been a vamp.

Gabby stood among the survivors, armed with her kukri and pistol and covered in blood that I hoped wasn't hers. I recognized Bobby's 'thrope form standing next to her, scanning the room for threats along with his packmates.

"Gabby, sitrep!" I yelled as I approached the group.

She lowered her weapons, but kept looking around as she replied. "As far as I know, we're the only survivors. Everyone was sacked out, but Bobby and I stayed up playing cards in the mess. One minute we were playing rummy, and the next the vamps swooped in, killing everyone in sight."

"Any threats besides the vamps?"

She shrugged. "About a dozen deaders that I saw, and a bunch of those deader dogs. We took out the hounds and deaders, but the vamps were a little tougher than I expected. We only got one of them, but they got one of the Pack, too."

One of the 'thropes howled a mournful cry that ran chills down my spine. I looked at the werewolf and gave what I hoped was an expression of sympathy. "I agree, but we can count our dead later. Right now, we need to find out how they got in and seal that opening. Bobby, take a team and find the breech, then secure it. Lock it up tight if you can, and if you can't, stay on guard at that exit."

He nodded and signaled to two wolves, and they bounded out of the room. "Gabby, you're with me." I looked at the remaining four 'thropes. "I could use one more, if that's alright."

A shorter werewolf with dark fur stepped forward. "I'm game. What's the plan?" I recognized Trina's voice—albeit a huskier, gravellier version of it.

"We need to do a sweep for any survivors, as well as any remaining threats. I'll need the rest of your packmates to stay here to guard the remaining survivors."

The half-dozen women and children who were left were obviously scared, but several had armed themselves. The fact that they weren't going to go down easily triggered something inside me. I got a nod from a large 'thrope in response to my request, and I took off out of the mess hall with Gabby and Trina behind me.

We checked every hall and room—even the armory, which had been locked up. Along the way, we killed a few deaders and a deader dog who was chewing a corpse all to hell. The attack had come in through a single access point, an emergency escape hatch that could only have been opened from the inside. The hatch itself had been ripped off the hinges, so we'd have to weld it shut once daylight came.

Bobby and his packmates were guarding the breached hatch when we finished our sweep. Bobby waved me over and led me to a nearby storage room. Inside, Nadine laid on a pallet made from metal storage boxes, bleeding from several nasty vamp bites.

"We found her like this, near the breach," Bobby said.

Unlike the vamps in the movies, these things didn't leave

two neat little holes that healed up with a lick. The woman had been savaged on one side of her neck, at the fossa inside the elbow joint of each arm, and inside her left thigh. How she was even still alive was a mystery to me, but I suspected it had something to do with the vyrus. She'd turn once she died, for sure.

I walked up and touched her shoulder, and her eyes blinked open in response. "Nadine, what happened? Did they break in on their own?"

The accusation was plain in my voice.

"I... I thought they just wanted you," she whispered. "They said they only wanted you."

"Damn it, Nadine—if they'd have wanted me, they would've killed me back in Austin when they had the chance."

"Didn't... know. How many died?"

I hung my head and squeezed the bridge of my nose. "A lot. Maybe half the survivors, in fact."

She squeezed her eyes shut. "Kill me."

"Oh, I intend to, but not as punishment for what you did. You're infected, and you'll turn once your heart doesn't have enough blood to pump. Maybe you'll become a deader, or maybe something worse like a ghoul or a rev. I can't let that happen."

"S—sorry. So sorry. Do it."

I drew my sidearm and held it to the side of her head. "Sorry won't be bring anyone back, but I'll tell them you said so."

She closed her eyes, and a tear ran down her cheek. I looked away and pulled the trigger.

THE ONE BIT of good news was that Mickey, Anna, and half their Wild Boys had barricaded themselves inside a room, while Colin had somehow managed to hold off any and all comers. I raised an eyebrow at the scorch marks and weird symbols on the wall, floor, and ceiling in the hall outside, but kept my comments to myself. I suspected that the big swordsman and Rabbi Borovitz had a lot in common, and intended to ask him about it in private.

Despite the heroic efforts of all involved, the losses we suffered in the attack were devastating. If Bobby's Pack hadn't been around when it happened... well, it would've been much worse. I hadn't been close to many of the settlers or LARPers, but I had gotten to know several of them since we'd taken out the Corridor Pack. Cleaning up after the fight and gathering their corpses for burial was a difficult and trying task.

Gabby's dog, Ghost, had also gone missing in the attack. We didn't find a body, so I assumed he'd been taken to become another of the witch's familiars. Gabby refused to discuss it.

During the aftermath of the attack, the hardest bit was

when I came across Janie's broken, mutilated body. She had run the general store back at the settlement, before the 'thropes had come through looking for Kara. Our interactions had always been friendly and somewhat flirtatious, and to be honest I'd have probably been with her if I wasn't already attached.

She'd been bitten and drained by a vamp, and after that her body had been torn apart by deader dogs and deaders. I took the sole responsibility of gathering up what was left of her to place it in a body bag for a proper burial. And if I wept a little while I did it—well, there was a lot of that going around, so I don't think anyone noticed.

I was cleaning Janie's blood off the floor when the Doc came running down the hall toward me. The Doc never really hurried to get anywhere, so I knew she was bringing me bad news.

"Scratch, we have a serious issue."

I looked her straight in the eye as I leaned on my mop. "New day, new crisis. Tell me what's up."

"It's the pest control system—it's been sabotaged. We already have undead roaming the area topside in singles and small groups."

"Shit—well, it's not like it's something we're not used to dealing with. How'd they break the damned thing, anyway? In fact, how'd they even know about it?"

"The system works as an ultra-high frequency sound emitter, similar to the way an ultrasonic dog bark controller operates. Except, instead of emitting a single high-frequency tone, the pest control system sends out a continuous series of commands—the same way a powerful vamp can give off messages that keep deaders away from their lair. I would imagine that one of the vamps detected the signal and trashed the emitters topside."

I stuck the mop I'd been using back in the bucket, doing my best to ignore how the water had turned brown with blood and other filth I'd had to clean up. "Damn it—do we have replacements, or a backup?"

"None. The system was experimental when we brought it online after the invasion occurred. It's one of a kind, I'm afraid."

"Has the hatch they breached been welded shut yet?"

She shook her head. "Not yet. Everyone has been too busy taking care of their dead."

I growled with exasperation. "Alright, then have the wolves replace the hatch and cover it with boulders from the outside, and I'll weld it shut myself as soon as I finish here. We can barricade that hall as an additional safety measure, and that should keep the deaders out for now."

She crossed her arms and rubbed her cheek with one hand. For the first time, I noticed deep circles under her eyes and worry lines on her face. "The real problem is, they know exactly where we are. What's to stop them from coming back and ripping open another hatch?"

I ran my fingers through my hair and scratched my head as I made an effort to clear the mental cobwebs away. Lack of sleep was affecting my ability to reason. *At least my deader bite isn't hurting as badly*, I thought.

"I don't have an answer to that question, but we can ask Samson or Colin about that, since they've dealt with these things before. For now, let's secure this place from the most immediate threat, then we can figure out how to go on the offensive."

She exhaled heavily, her mouth taut with worry. "If it helps, I can vaccinate anyone who volunteers. We can consider it a field test, I suppose."

"We might have to go further than that, Doc."

"You mean dose them with serum?"

I shrugged. "Sure, why not? You've seen how these things

move, and how dangerous they are—don't you think those people deserve every advantage possible to survive?"

She stared at me, long and hard, then finally her shoulders slumped slightly. "I suppose you're right. But Tony and I agreed long ago that anyone who got the serum needed to be vetted carefully. It's a lot of power to put in the wrong hands, Scratch."

Tony had been Gabby's uncle. I'd never gotten the full details on how he fit into everything, but from the way the kid talked about him, I'd guessed he was a spook before the War. Probably complicit in all their secret testing here at the Facility, too. Gabby had said he'd disappeared after they'd gotten jumped by 'thropes, right before I'd rescued her.

Or before she'd rescued me. It was a matter of perspective, I supposed.

I returned the Doc's stare, chewing my lip as I considered my words. "When the choices are evolution or extinction, Lorena, is there really any choice at all?"

She took a deep breath and closed her eyes as she let it out slowly. It was clear that this was a tough decision for her. Her eyes popped open as she replied. "Again, you're right. But it may not take with everyone—you realize that, don't you?"

"Doc, if we only had half our people juiced, it'd make a huge difference in our chances for survival. Do it."

I heard a deep voice bellow from somewhere down the hallway, shortly after the 'thropes had secured the broken hatch from the outside. "Who the hell is responsible for allowing the fucking undead—and civilians—into my secure top-secret facility?"

Gabby was standing nearby, and I noticed she perked up at the sound of that voice. "Uncle Tony?" she asked in a loud but tremulous voice.

A lean but solidly built Hispanic man in his early forties strolled around the corner. He had a scarred face that made mine look pretty, short dark hair, and serious, deep set brown eyes. The man had a pair of H&K forty-five caliber pistols strapped to his hips, an M4 rifle slung over one shoulder, and some sort of cutlass or machete scabbarded over the other. He stood about five-foot-ten and had the look of a stone killer. *Definitely a spook,* I thought.

He locked eyes with Gabby and gave her a nod. "Hey there, *mija*. Glad to see you're doing okay."

Gabby marched up to him and slapped him across the face. *Hard.* Then, she shoved him with enough force to make him stumble. "You asshole! I thought you were dead. And you left me alone out there, you son of a bitch!"

Then she was hugging him fiercely, pressing her face into his chest and soaking his green BDU shirt with her tears. The man was obviously uncomfortable with the display of affection, but he began stroking her hair and whispering in her ear.

"Hey now, that's no way to speak of your *abuela, mija*. If she were here she'd wash your mouth out with soap." The kid leaned back as if to slap him again, and he smiled and held his hands up. "Relax, Gabby. I'm here now, and that's all that matters, right?"

She hugged him again, then backed off stiffly. She glanced at me before looking away shyly, wiping her eyes where I couldn't see. Finally, she composed herself and stood between us in an awkward stance, the way only a teenager could manage.

"Scratch, this is my Uncle Tony."

I nodded. The man looked at me and half-smiled, half-frowned—an impossible expression that seemed natural to him. "I see you found our lab rat, *mija. Hay chingao,* but he looks like he's been through the wringer."

I kept my face and voice neutral as I replied. "Right back at you, pretty boy. Now that I've met you in person, I can see why you and the Doc get along so well. Between the two of you, you might actually have a whole personality."

He looked at Gabby quizzically. "The Doc?"

"He means Aunt Lorena."

"Ah." The man nodded, then stepped forward and held out a hand. "Thanks for looking after my niece while I was gone."

I had my reservations about this guy, but for Gabby's sake I shook his hand. "She looked after me as much as I did her."

"That doesn't surprise me. It's the last order I gave her before we parted ways."

"The last thing you told me was to run, *pendejo*," she said with a frown.

He shrugged, almost imperceptibly. "Yeah, but you knew we were looking for Sergeant Sullivan. He was the last surviving test subject from the initial Cerberus trials." Tony looked at me and smirked. "Looks like getting your ass blown off in Afghanistan worked to your favor, Sullivan. If you hadn't, you'd have probably been with the rest of the test subjects when our base got overrun by the dead."

"Lucky me."

"Yeah, well—I know you probably have your panties in a wad over being left in the dark, but you know how Uncle Sam operates. Everything is 'need to know,' and a soldier doesn't need to know shit. Besides, the serum you got is a lot more... stable, if that's the right word. Some of those boys went batshit crazy after we juiced them. Not a pretty sight. Believe me, you pulled a long straw."

"How'd you know I took the serum?" I asked.

"The same way I knew this facility had been compromised. Been monitoring what's been going on all along. We have facilities like this all over Texas—and most of the continental United States. Or what's left of it. Damned shame about the pest control system, though. That tech'll be hard to duplicate for a while yet."

I rubbed my bite scar unconsciously as I spoke. "How much of the old government structure is still in place?"

"I can't talk about that. Not yet, anyway. And before you ask, I can't divulge the location of the other secure facilities, either. Vamps have been looking for them since they dropped the bombs on us." I raised an eyebrow at him. "Oh yeah, they were responsible for that. Bloodsuckers had infiltrated key nuclear facilities the world over through their familiars."

"You mean those dog things we've been fighting?" I asked.

He gave his niece a look that said I was the slow kid in class. "Huh? Good night, but you're clueless. No, with people. Vamps feed on them and they gain a sort of mind control over them. It's subtle, but it becomes stronger over time. And then there are humans who want to get turned. Those worthless pricks will do anything for a shot at immortality.

"Once they had all their people in place, all they had to do was release a few warheads, and we stepped in to do the rest. It's just sheer luck that we figured it out in time to avoid mutual, worldwide nuclear destruction."

I crossed my arms. "Thanks for the illuminating history lesson, but why are you really here?"

"Besides the fact that you people exposed the location of this facility to the enemy... and you allowed them to get inside?" He leaned in close as he spoke in a whisper. "A working vaccine, Sergeant Sullivan. That's what the future hope of the entire world hinges upon. And I'm not about to let you and your gang of misfits fuck things up by letting it fall into the enemy's hands."

Colin and I were aboveground and outside the Facility, killing any deaders we came across. It was a losing battle, but we weren't trying to clear the area. We were only clearing the way from one hidden entrance to another, so Colin could "ward" the hatches and doors—whatever the hell that meant.

"You're telling me the squiggly lines and shit you're drawing are supposed to keep vamps out?"

"Uh-huh," he said as he traced impossibly intricate symbols on the surface of a metal hatch. He'd somehow found a bunch of permanent markers that hadn't dried out, though I had no idea how. He furrowed his brow in concentration as he worked, and while I doubted the efficacy of the drawings, I appreciated the effort.

"What does it do, scare them away or something?"

"Or something," he mumbled as he continued drawing.

"I'd rather just set up claymores and IEDs at all the entrances."

"Yeah, but you and I both know the dead would only set them off, then the vamps would know where every entrance to the Facility was located."

I picked up a good-sized rock and chucked it at a deader's head that had popped up over a nearby rise. The rock hit the thing cleanly in the temple, dropping it. It did not get back up.

"I know. I just think good old-fashioned munitions are more reliable than all this mumbo-jumbo."

"Meh, it depends on the enemy. If we were just dealing with normal humans, I'd probably advise going your route. But against vamps? Trust me, you fight the supernatural with the supernatural, whenever possible."

Two more deaders came over the rise, moaning and groaning as soon as they saw us. The ruckus they made wasn't loud enough to bring more of their kind to investigate, but they'd locked in on us. I loosened my sword in its scabbard as I kept an eye on them.

"You just about done?" I said as I unsheathed my sword. We'd been at it for a few hours, and while the scar from my deader bite didn't hurt near as bad, my arms and shoulders were fatigued from lopping heads off.

"Just about," he replied, sticking his tongue out the side of his mouth as he finished drawing an intricate series of circles, loop-the-loops, and squiggly lines on the hatch.

The deaders were nearly on us. I stepped forward almost casually and chopped their heads off, then snapped the sword out and to the side to sling most of the goo off the blade. I wiped it down with a few dried leaves, but kept it out as a precaution. I scanned our perimeter, just in case more of the dead showed.

"How are you dealing with your losses?"

He stopped drawing for a moment as he looked down at the ground. "I'd rather not talk about it."

"Alright." I turned away from him, and ignored the tingling up my spine that was accompanied by a flash of light behind me. *Nope, I don't want to know.* I heard a bit of rustling as Colin stood up.

"Done. That should keep the vamps from ripping off another hatch. If they touch any of these entrances, they're going to get the shock of their undead lives."

"If you say so. But it still doesn't mean they can't come down here with high explosives, or tanks, or an RPG, and just blow the flipping place wide open."

He nodded. "True. Anonymity and secrecy were our best defenses."

"I should have kicked Nadine out at the first sign of trouble."

"And then what? She'd have run straight to the vamps, told them everything about the Facility and how to get inside, and then we'd be in the same predicament. C'mon, man, we can't go second-guessing ourselves right now. We need to be thinking proactively, and planning a way to defeat the vamps for good."

I sat on a fallen log and rested the sword across my knees. "I suppose the vaccine is a start."

Colin sat on the same log, a couple of feet away and facing the opposite direction. "It is at that. How many of the survivors have taken it so far?"

"All of them, I think. We had one anaphylactic reaction, but the Doc dosed them with epinephrine and antihistamines and they pulled through." I kicked over a leaf, revealing a large red centipede underneath. "I notice you haven't had it yet."

"Don't need it. I'm... uh... immune."

"More mumbo-jumbo?"

"Yep."

We sat there in silence for several minutes, just enjoying the scenery. Except for the moans and groans of deaders in the distance, I could almost imagine I was camping out at the ranch, before the War and subsequent undead apocalypse.

"Colin, shoot me straight."

"Sure, Scratch."

"If they come at us with everything they've got, do we even have a chance?"

He thought for a moment as he nudged a stone with his boot. "Not a snowball's chance in hell. The ones that attacked us last night were young, and not so hard to kill. If they really want us dead, they'll come with dozens of primaries, ancient vampires like Piotr with powers that absolutely dwarf our meager skills and talents. I tried fighting a vamp like that once, with another powerful but younger vampire beside me. It wasn't even a contest... not even close."

"So, we're pretty much fucked."

"Yup. May as well change your name to Mike Honcho and spread your butt cheeks for *Playgirl* magazine."

I laughed in spite of myself. Cracking jokes in the face of certain death was a universal characteristic among warriors.

"Man, I miss Will Ferrell movies."

"You and me both."

THE VAMPS CAME AGAIN the next night, and the night after that. Best we could tell, Colin's hoodoo was working. We'd hear a pop and hiss outside a door or hatch in the dead of the night, and then the next day we'd find pieces of vamp all over the place.

Still, they kept coming.

Tony had already left to parts unknown, along with a sample of the vaccine and a copy of the Doc's research. He at least had the decency to say goodbye to his niece before he left, so I had to give him that. But when I'd mentioned that we could sure use his help when the vamps showed up in force, he'd laughed and simply said, "Yeah, good luck with that."

I was happy to see him go. But he did leave me a present, something he said was a "break glass in case of emergency" kind of thing. It looked like those atropine auto-injectors they used to give soldiers, that you were supposed to self-inject if you were exposed to chemical weapons. Everybody knew they would only keep us fighting a few minutes longer, although we were told it was a life-saving measure.

"What the hell is this?" I asked.

"It's something the lab geeks cooked up," he said, "for Cerberus operatives—soldiers like you and me who made it through the trials. Command knew that even with the serum we couldn't go toe-to-toe with the worst things that are out there. Ancient vamps and 'thropes, *oni*, liches, and the like. So, they had the eggheads cook up a sort of booster serum for us. It's like adrenaline on crack. It'll burst your fucking heart if you're not careful, but if you gotta go out in a blaze of glory, well"—he shrugged—"injecting that shit will make it happen."

I tucked the injector in my pocket. "Thanks, I guess."

He chuckled. "Soldier, trust me—if you have to use it, the last thing you'll be doing is thanking me." He shouldered his ruck and headed down the hall toward the exit without another word.

What a dick, I thought.

We kept the place locked up tight most of the time. There wasn't any sense in running patrols outside, since the area was overrun by deaders during the day and infested with blood-suckers at night. We had the whole Coastal Pack living in there, along with what remained of the settlers, Colin and his LARPers, plus the Doc, Bobby, Gabby, and me. Being shut in and under the constant threat of death left everyone on edge, and the natives were getting restless.

The LARPers wanted to go back to Austin. The settlers wanted to head out west, find some land that was relatively free of deaders, and start over. The 'thropes were ready to head back to the coast, and say screw the Dallas coven. And honestly, I couldn't blame any of them. Hell, I wanted to cut and run myself.

But the reality was that Calypso and her brood were hanging close. The minute any of us made a break for it, she'd hunt them down. I figured she had a lair somewhere nearby, close enough to keep an eye on us, but far enough away to make it difficult for us to find. And at the rate she was throwing vamps at us, I also suspected she was grabbing punters and scavs and turning them in order to add to her ranks.

She wouldn't come at us hard, not yet. Not until Kara turned up. I think she believed that if I was in enough danger, eventually my ex would show up and try to save me. Seemed like a gamble to me, but Calypso must have been sure of herself, otherwise she'd have high-tailed it back to Dallas with all the intel she'd collected. Then it'd all be over, for all of us—vaccine or no.

With nowhere to go, I spent a lot of time waiting, healing, training, and thinking. Calypso was making a tactical error by not leaving with that intel, and I kept trying to figure out a way to use it against her. After several days of contemplating our situation, I hatched a plan... but I only revealed part of it to the others.

Early one morning, I gathered everybody in the mess hall to address them. Not just the key players, but everyone, because everyone was going to have a role to play if we were going to pull this freaking thing off. Besides, the Doc had been juicing anyone who'd take the serum, and while she only had about a fifty-five percent success rate, the ones it had worked on were champing at the bit.

Between the juiced LARPers and settlers, the 'thropes, Colin's voodoo, and myself, I gave us a fifty-fifty chance of survival against Calypso and her vamps. It'd have to do.

I stood in front of everyone and addressed them with as much presence as I could muster. "Folks, you all know we're stuck between a rock and a hard place. That bloodsucking witch and her vamps are out there, waiting for us to make a wrong move."

"Don't forget the deader dogs," Bobby interjected. Gabby

nudged him in the ribs. "What? They're creepy and hard to kill. I just didn't want anyone to forget."

"No one can forget those *perros* from hell, *payaso!*" she hissed. "Now be quiet, for once."

I cleared my throat. "As I was saying, we're kind of stuck here. We have enough food to feed everyone for maybe a month, maybe less. Hunting has become harder to do, since the vamps are herding the undead toward us at night, leaving the area aboveground swarming with cold bodies."

"Who kill and eat anything that moves," Mickey muttered, "including wild game."

"That's right," I said. "Meaning foraging and hunting are no longer practical survival strategies. We can't stay here much longer, because we're going to run out of food. And we can't leave, because except for the 'thropes, none of us can get far enough away from here in a single day to avoid being slaughtered by Calypso and her brood."

Samson spoke up from the back, where he was leaning against the wall like a statue. "We're not abandoning anyone."

He looked at his adopted son, and I got his meaning clearly. He was staying because Bobby was staying. I wondered how long it'd be before he had a mutiny on his hands. That was one of the reasons I had decided to make a move. I needed the Coastal Pack backing my play if it was going to succeed.

"I appreciate that, Samson. Really, I do. But if we keep ourselves locked up inside here, we're just sitting ducks. Eventually Calypso will wear down Colin's traps, or she'll find a way to break through them—"

Colin cut me off. "She's been working on it, believe me. They'll hold, for a time, but eventually she'll get through."

"Right," I continued. "So, we either wait and allow ourselves to get slaughtered, or we take the fight to her."

Anna addressed me directly from the front row. "Scratch,

we don't even know where she's hiding out." She turned to face the rest of the group. "I'm all for going down fighting, but if we just run around out there blind, she'll pick us off one by one."

I nodded. "Exactly right. So, we find her lair, and then we go there during the day and take her out."

"Didn't you already try that?" one of the settlers said.

"I did, but I didn't know what I was up against. Now I do. And if we attack during the day, chances are good that most of her vamps will be resting and dormant. Hopefully we'll only have to deal with her, and maybe one or two others."

Samson nodded. "The numbers seem to be in our favor. But just how do you plan on dealing with Calypso herself? From what I gather, she's a primary. They eat hunters and 'thropes and shit them out for fun."

I didn't want to tell them how I intended to deal with her, but I had a plan. It was a gamble, but I thought it might work. "Don't worry about Calypso, because I'll be handling her."

Colin looked at me like I was insane, but he kept his mouth shut. There was some grumbling from a few of the others, but for the most part people were nodding their heads and agreeing with me.

"So then, it's settled. First, we locate their lair—then, we take the fight to them."

Colin cornered me in an empty hallway, soon after everyone who had attended the meeting had dispersed. "What's this bullshit about you taking out Calypso on your own?"

I motioned for him to follow me into an empty office, and closed the door behind us. "Look, I know it sounds crazy, but trust me—I have a plan."

"A plan to get yourself killed."

"I'll admit that the odds are stacked against me. But if the Dallas coven gets their hands on all that enriched plutonium buried at Pantex, we're going to be royally and completely screwed. We have to stop Calypso—not just because she's a threat to the group, but because we need to keep that intel out of the vamps' hands."

He rubbed his forehead and growled. "I can't believe I'm agreeing with you on this, but you're right. Still, someone in Dallas is going to know if we take Calypso off the board... her master or one of her broodmates. Vamps are weird like that— sort of semi-telepathic where their offspring and siblings are concerned. They will come at us in force, Scratch. You can count on it."

"We'll just have to cross that bridge when we get to it. Let's deal with one crisis at a time."

"If you say so."

"Anyway, the first step is to track her back to wherever she's been hiding out. I need you to take one of your Wild Boys who got juiced and a 'thrope, and work the western sectors to see if you can find a scent trail back to their lair. I'll take Bobby and Gabby to check the east side of the base. We'll meet back here tonight and compare notes."

The big swordsman pursed his lips, then nodded. "Consider it done. Just be sure you don't try to take on Calypso and her brood if you find them before I do."

"Not a chance; not with the kids with me. We'll attack them in force, when we're damned good and ready."

"Alright then. Happy hunting." Colin gave me a half-assed, pseudo-military salute and headed off to gather his people. I sat on the desk in the office, taking a moment to consider the situation at hand before I did the same.

There was more to my plan than what I was telling him. For example, I intended to haul ass away from the group if Calypso opted to escape rather than fight. That would at least take the heat off everyone else, but I couldn't let them know my intentions. Otherwise, Bobby, Gabby, and maybe even Colin or the Doc might decide to tag along. No way I'd let that happen.

I also already had a plan to deal with the Dallas coven, after we handled Calypso and her followers. It was sketchy, at best, but I was fairly certain I could make it work with the Doc's help. But first, we had to find Calypso.

Bobby and Gabby were standing outside the office door when I exited. Gabby had her hands on her hips and was giving me the evil eye, while Bobby was whistling and trying to look like they hadn't been eavesdropping.

"Cut the act, Bobby. I know you guys were listening in on our discussion."

Gabby tongued her cheek and sighed angrily. "I don't know if I'm more pissed that you still insist on referring to us as 'kids,' or that you're planning on sacrificing yourself for the group."

I shrugged. "It's kind of become my hobby. Anyway, I have a plan."

Bobby threw his hands up in the air. "You always have a plan, Scratch. And that's what worries me."

I started walking down the hall to get my gear, and they followed behind. "Like I told Colin, let's deal with one crisis at a time. The first order of business is finding Calypso, so grab your shit and let's move out."

Gabby caught up to me and smirked. "We're already geared up, because we know how you think. Well, I'm geared up, anyway—all wolf boy here seems to think he needs is a pair of board shorts and some Vans."

"Hey, don't bust on me for bucking the post-apocalyptic, Mad Max, paramilitary fashion thing everybody seems to have going on. I may not look good in camo, but I can rock a pair of board shorts and a Hawaiian shirt."

"And the enemy can see you coming from a mile away, *estúpido*."

Bobby pulled out a cheap pair of neon orange sunglasses and put them on. "Shee-it, I'm so smooth, nobody sees me coming if I don't want them to."

Gabby rolled her eyes. "Yeah, you're right—they smell you coming long before they see you, *perro*."

Twenty minutes later, we were outside the Facility and running a sweep of the eastern perimeter. We'd started by checking every exit on the eastern side of the Facility, especially those that we knew the vamps had tried to breach. Picking up a trail was tricky, because the vamps were highly intelligent and knew how to avoid leaving signs of their passage.

I suspected that the farther out we went, the more likely we were to find a trail, as they'd probably be less careful farther away from the Facility. And I was right. We picked up a trail about a mile from the southernmost exit.

Bobby was down on all fours, sniffing the ground around a tree nearby. "Sneaky bastards. Looks like they've been jumping from tree to tree to avoid leaving a scent on the ground."

I knelt down to look at the trail he'd picked up, and followed it further southwest with my eyes. "Let's see where it leads."

It didn't take us long to figure out that we were headed straight toward the hospital where we'd first ran into Bobby's Pack.

Gabby gave me a knowing look. "You thinking what I'm thinking?"

"The tunnel we saw in the elevator shaft? Yeah, that's what I was thinking. I bet we were right on top of one of her lairs the whole time, and didn't even know it."

When we got within a mile or so of the hospital, we spotted a deader dog patrol. Calypso was using them to monitor and guard her lair during the day, just as she had back at the Reserve Center. I motioned for the kids to hide until they passed.

"Colin mentioned that it's possible she can see what they see," I said. "So, it's imperative that we don't get spotted. And we can't leave a scent trail they can pick up, either. They'll know we were here, and Calypso will move her lair."

Bobby looked at me and tilted his head like a dog. "What's our play, boss?"

"We need to confirm that they're hiding out in the hospital. But if we don't make it back to the Facility by the time Colin and his team return, they're going to come looking for us."

Gabby frowned and looked at Bobby. "This is the part where he gets rid of us so he can hatch one of his suicidal plans."

I sighed. "I'm not going to try to take out Calypso on my own. But I do need you two to head back to the Facility to let them know what we found. Meanwhile, I'm going to find someplace nice, high, and secluded, where I can keep an eye on the hospital from a distance. I'll stay out of sight and head back in the morning to let you know if our hunch is right."

"One of us should stay with you," Bobby said.

"Nope. One person can hide their scent, but two or more might get detected. We can't risk it, so just listen to me for once, alright? I'll be fine, trust me."

"Famous last words," Gabby muttered. "C'mon, wolf boy, let's head back and tell *el caballero* what we found."

"The cowboy?" Bobby asked with a confused expression.

"That's a *vaquero*, dummy. A *caballero* is a knight."

"She means Colin," I said.

"Oh... right!" He raised a finger in the air. "Hey, we should all get code names. That way, if we're overheard, our enemies won't know what we're talking about."

"I vote that you should be *culero*," Gabby said, deadpan. "Scratch, we'll see you back home in the morning. Be safe." She'd already started heading back, while Bobby considered her suggestion.

"Cool Arrow? I like it! But what should we call you?" The kid was so lost in thought, it took him a moment to realize she'd left him behind. When he did, he gave me a wave before running after her. The pair continued arguing at a whisper as they disappeared into the brush.

I waited until they were long gone, then found a relatively fresh deader wandering alone. I lured it into a building, where I killed it and used its guts to cover my scent. After I'd disguised my human odor with deader scent, I looped around in a wide arc—south, then east, then north. Finally, I headed back toward the hospital from the eastern side, where I suspected the vamps' patrols would be light.

I was correct, and managed to make it to an office building about a mile from the hospital undetected. From there, I'd set up on one of the upper floors and observe the area. If the hospital actually was Calypso's hideout, I'd find out soon enough after dark.

Despite the presence of the deader dogs in the area, there were plenty of undead inside the building when I entered. I had no idea whether they'd ignore me, now that my body was getting my deader infection under control. In any case, I needed those deaders left undisturbed, to avoid tipping off any vamps to my presence. I tapped on a window on the north side of the building to draw their attention, then snuck around the east side to peek through one of the main doors.

All clear. Moving as silently as possible, I searched the bottom floor until I found the stairs. I listened at the door and heard nothing but silence. I was picking up deader movement behind me, so I opened the door to the stairwell and quickly ducked inside.

Except for a small sliver of light coming from under the door, it was pitch dark inside. I waited by the door listening intently, cautious of a deader ambush. They might not have been able to infect me anymore, but a swarm could sure as hell chew me to bits.

As my enhanced vision adjusted to the gloom, two slender figures began to take shape on the landing above me. One was shorter, lean, and feminine, while the other was tall and almost skeletal in appearance. I blinked several times, trying to make sense of what I was seeing, and wondering if I was hallucinating.

A familiar whisper told me that my mind was definitely not playing tricks on me.

"Hey there, tall, scarred, and handsome... come here often?"

"KARA?" I whispered, dumbstruck.

"And your old chum, Donnie," another familiar and incredibly creepy voice replied. It sounded like dry leaves rubbing against a gravestone, with a faint echo underneath punctuating each syllable. "We've been keeping this lovely lady company, Scratch—I certainly hope you don't mind. You never struck me as the jealous type... no, not at all."

As my eyes fully adjusted to the thick darkness in the stairwell, the two figures before me came into focus. Kara was wearing jeans, work boots, a Johnny Cash t-shirt that was two sizes too small, and a leather bomber jacket. She had her auburn hair in a ponytail, pulled out the back of an Astros baseball cap. Her right hand held the barrel of a Barrett .50 caliber sniper rifle, and her left rested on the hilt of heavy machete.

She looked beautiful... and heartbreakingly undead.

Donnie the Wendigo, on the other hand, was dressed like an undertaker. He'd grown taller, and leaner as well, if that were possible. His skin was stretched tautly over his skeleton and whatever scraps of sinew and muscle held him together. He wore a tattered black suit with coattails, over an equally ratty black vest, filthy white dress shirt, moth-eaten charcoal slacks, and black dress shoes that had seen better days. His eyes were black orbs that sat deeply in their sockets like two dark gemstones. As he spoke, his breath smelled like fetid water and decomposition, and he revealed a mouthful of needle-sharp teeth when he smiled.

As I looked the pair over, feelings of anger and frustration mixed with longing and regret inside me. For lack of a better coping mechanism, I chose to focus on the anger. Anger was better than hurt or regret, any day of the week.

"It's been a while, Scratch old buddy, yes indeed it has." The wendigo took a long pull at the air between us through nostrils that were nothing more than two narrow openings in his skeletal face. "You're looking well, and smelling a bit less... infected? Pestilent? Biohazardous? Kudos to Captain Perez for managing to keep you alive this long."

I ignored the revolting creature, choosing instead to focus my attention on Kara. "What the hell are you two doing here?"

"The same as you, apparently. We've been staking out Calypso's lair, waiting for an opportunity to take her out." She cocked an ear, as if listening to something at a distance. "Let's move upstairs. I don't want one of her patrols to hear us. The last thing we need is for that bitch to come storming through here like hell's own fury."

"After you." I took a deep breath and let it out slowly as I looked at Donnie. "That means both of you. I'm not about to turn my back on you—or her, for that matter."

Donnie stepped back, pulling himself up to his full height as he laid a hand on his chest with an effete grace. "Why, Scratch, I would never—"

I held up a hand. "Save it, Donnie. I don't have the patience for your bullshit today."

Kara narrowed her eyes at me. "If I'd wanted to eat you, I'd have done it back at the research campus. This way, please." She made her way up the stairs, completely silent. Although her pace was almost languid, she took the stairs two and three at a time, moving weightlessly as her vampire physiology defied gravity and the laws of physics.

I waited until Donnie followed her before I did the same. He took the steps one at time, despite the fact that he could have easily leapt from one landing to the next in a single bound. I'd seen him perform incredible feats of agility, including dodging gunfire, so I was certain he was taking his sweet time just to get a rise from me. Instead of taking the bait, I checked the door to make sure it was closed and latched, then headed up after them.

We stopped at the thirteenth floor, just one floor from the top level. *Fitting.* Kara opened the exit door soundlessly, and I noted someone had oiled the hinges recently. She led us to a conference room at the center of the floor, sticking to the shadows and avoiding any and all reflected sunlight along the way. She lit a kerosene lamp and adjusted the wick so it gave off only the tiniest bit of light. The light was for me, not her, but I chose to overlook the gesture.

Donnie leapt atop the conference table, landing in a handstand. He had to fold his legs to avoid hitting the rotting ceiling tiles above us as he walked on his hands to the other side of the table. Once there, he crossed his legs like a swami and rested his head on the table. Then he folded his arms across his chest, balancing perfectly in that crazy headstand as he hummed "Ring Around the Rosie."

Kara pulled out a chair for me, but I looked at her and shook my head.

"I'll stand, I think." I leaned against the wall just inside the doorway, where I could keep an eye on them both and make a fast exit. Not that I thought I could do anything to either of them if they decided to hurt me; I just wanted to feel like I had options.

She shrugged and sat in the chair she'd pulled out. "Suit yourself." Kara leaned back, legs extended and ankles crossed, with her fingers intertwined over her flat stomach. "You're angry with me... or maybe you're angry at yourself for letting me get turned. Get over it, Scratch. We have bigger problems right now, and one of them is sitting in an earthen tunnel forty feet beneath that hospital."

***

I had to admit, talking to my undead ex was a little unsettling. And yeah, I was feeling more than a small bit of anger, both at myself for failing to save her, and at her for being an undeniable reminder that I'd come up short in my efforts. But she was right; being a dick wasn't going to help matters. And while I couldn't fully trust her—now that she was a vampire—I still loved her. That would never change.

So, I decided that I might as well act like it.

"My apologies for being a little on edge. I just—"

"Never expected to see me again?"

I nodded. "There is that."

She tapped her thumbs together and stared at me for a moment. "I'll admit, after we parted ways I considered ending my own life. And, to be honest, I fully intended to stay away from you. You're a hunter, Scratch, through and through. You kill the undead for a living, and I'm... well, what I am is obvious. That's a recipe for disaster if ever I heard one."

"And yet, here we are."

"Here we are."

I raised my chin in Donnie's direction. "How'd you get mixed up with him?"

The corners of her mouth turned up in a rueful smile. "He found me shortly after I left you at the research center, and now I can't get rid of him. Donnie's annoying as hell and more than a little creepy, but he's helped me understand my... condition. And, he's managed to keep Calypso from finding me. We've been right under her nose since she arrived from Dallas, yet thus far we've escaped detection."

"Any idea how Fruit Loops fooled the witch?"

Kara's brow furrowed, at least as much as her perfect vampire skin would allow. "Magic, I suppose. It's like the vamps can't even see me, much less pick up my scent when he's around."

"You do know what he is, right?"

She pursed her lips and nodded. "And he knows what I am. Hasn't seemed to faze him any, unlike some other people I know." *Ouch.* "Besides, he says he prefers the taste of punter. I think he's drawn to them, actually—cannibals, I mean."

"And you?"

"I feed when he feeds. I drain them and he finishes the job, so no one comes back. It's an arrangement that's worked thus far."

I searched her face for some sign of deceit, and saw none. "And what about your thirst? Is it controlled? Do you want to drain me, right now?"

"No, Scratch, I don't. As long as I feed every few days, the urges are manageable." She glanced over her shoulder at Donnie, who was still balancing on his head humming nursery rhymes. "Piotr told me that before the War, vampires lived hidden among us, and many of them chose to feed only on volunteers. They took just enough to survive, and went to great lengths to avoid killing those who volunteered to feed them. I asked Donnie if it was true, and he confirmed it. Not all vamps are killers, Scratch."

I scowled. "Piotr controlled your mind, robbing you of your free will. And Donnie here is more than a little loony, if you hadn't noticed. Between the two of them you might have gotten a sliver of the whole truth."

Donnie piped up from the far end of the room. "While I might be mentally unstable, I've never lied to you, Scratch. And neither have I misled the lovely Kara. She speaks the truth."

I pointed a finger at the wendigo. "Donnie, stay out of this," I growled. I turned back to Kara. "I suppose the subtext here is that you and I can just pick up where we left off? That we can live happily ever after, like a couple of characters in a Scandinavian horror film?"

She closed her eyes and lowered her chin slightly. "You're right. Forget I said anything," she whispered. After a few moments, she opened her eyes and turned her gaze westward. "Now, tell me your grand plan for stopping Calypso."

"Why? Are you planning on helping me?"

She gave me a look that I recognized, one that said she was losing her patience. "I told you why we're here. We've been looking for a chance to plant seven hundred grains of copper-encased silver in her chest. Unfortunately, that opportunity hasn't presented itself yet. Donnie says we need to be within a hundred feet of her, otherwise she'll dodge the shot."

"Since when did you become an expert sniper?"

She glanced down at the rifle, refusing to meet my eyes. "It's a vampire thing. Physical skills come easy to me, these days."

"At least one of us got something out of it," I whispered. I pretended I didn't see her wince at my words. "Vampire powers be damned, I don't see how Calypso can dodge a high-velocity projectile. She damned sure won't hear it coming—a fifty caliber sniper round travels at twice the speed of sound."

"Scratch, you may know a lot about hunting lesser vamps,

but you're not exactly an expert on creatures like Piotr. I once saw him dodge small arms fire at close range—"

"And you've seen me do it," Donnie interjected. "Trust me, the witch will pull a Neo, given the chance."

I turned toward the wendigo and scowled. "Just how in the hell do you know who Neo is?"

He tapped his skull. "Donnie still lives in here, remember? He says 'hi,' by the way." He cocked his head to the side. "What's that? Kill you? Well, that would mean killing *me*, my dear fellow. Besides, Scratch is no more capable of ending my life than he is of ending Calypso's. Stop being silly, Donnie."

I took a step toward him, fists clenched, but stopped myself. I counted to ten, then turned my attention back to Kara. "So, you can't get close enough without tipping your hand. Which means you need a distraction in order to cap the witch."

"We'd hoped you might help us with that... considering that she wants to kill us both."

I rubbed a hand across my forehead. "Two things. First, why doesn't Lurch over there take her out, if he's so interested in seeing her eat a bullet? And second, why don't you distract her and let me take the shot?"

She shook her head. "Donnie says he can't engage them directly. Something about a pact between his kind and theirs."

"Why does that not surprise me?" I shot the wendigo a sideways glance, and he winked at me. "And the other thing?"

"You'd never get close enough to score a hit. It's going to take another vampire to end her, and even with all my advantages, I still might miss. Of course, there's not a chance in hell you can distract her without getting yourself killed. We figured you could get the 'thropes to help you draw her out, or maybe herd her into the open."

"Unnecessary. She won't kill me, not unless she knows

you're there to watch it happen. She told me as much herself. Calypso wants to drain me right before your eyes, while you stand by, helpless to do anything to stop her. And based on what you've said, allowing her to feed on me might be our only option."

Donnie uncrossed his arms, using his hands to propel himself into a headspin, breakdancer style. He made several revolutions, then froze in a B-boy pose on his side before pushing himself to a cross-legged seated position. The wendigo cupped his hands over his mouth and mimicked a cheesy announcer's voice as he spoke.

"Once more, Scratch Sullivan risks life and limb to rescue his friends and companions from certain death at the hands of his supernatural adversaries. Tune in next week to find out if the ancient vampiric witch will bleed our intrepid hero dry, or if he'll somehow manage to pull off the upset of the century!"

"It does sound pretty suicidal," Kara added.

"Only if you don't shoot her before she can finish the job," I replied.

───

That night I stuck around, just as I'd originally planned, in order to verify Calypso's presence with my own eyes. Kara and Donnie hadn't lied. Shortly after complete darkness fell, she and dozens of her vamps flooded out of the hospital and headed straight for the Facility.

I knew what she was up to, because it had become a pattern over the last few weeks. She'd throw a couple of vamps at the doors to harass us and keep us underground, all while she chipped away at whatever hoodoo Colin had worked to prevent the vamps from bum-rushing the Facility again.

After I'd seen Calypso with my own eyes, I locked myself in

an office to get some sleep. Not that I thought a flimsy door and some drywall would keep Kara or Donnie out; I just wanted the extra few seconds to try to snap a shot off if one of them decided to eat me.

Neither of them bothered me during the night, but I still didn't manage to get much sleep. And the few hours I did get were filled with nightmares about Piotr turning Kara into a vamp, of Donnie eating everyone in the settlement, and of Calypso breaking into the Facility and turning everyone into deaders. The next morning, I woke up sore, tired, and in a pissy mood.

I exited the office and found a note taped to the door:

We decided it was best to move during the night while the witch and her offspring were away. Do what you have to do to draw her out in the open, and I'll take the shot. -K

I crumpled the note and tossed it aside, then thought better of it. Instead, I dumped out a metal trash can and lit the note on fire, then dropped it in the can. A few minutes later, I was geared up and heading back to the Facility.

Deaders were thick on the way back, even though I'd looped around from the west side. The good news was, they were still leaving me alone. They'd pick up movement from me, come to investigate, then take a sniff and turn around or just stand there looking confused. Make that more confused than usual, considering the decomposing brain thing and all.

There were deader dogs around as well, moving in singles and pairs as they ran patrols. I did my best to avoid being seen, although it was difficult. The damned things never made a sound, not a single growl or whimper. So, I had to keep my head on a swivel in order to spot them before they spotted me. I was hiding from a patrol inside an old Army office building on the base when I heard a familiar voice yelling nearby.

"You'll not get me, *alte makhsheyfe*—not with these pitiful creatures. Josef! Show the witch what a properly reanimated creature can do, *ja?*"

I glanced out the window and saw one half of a dog flying over a nearby building. *Has to be the rabbi*, I thought. I left my hiding place and ran toward the commotion.

I rounded a building to find the rabbi backed into the corner of a fenced-in area behind a warehouse. Josef was in front of him, swinging a metal light pole in broad arcs to keep a group of a dozen or so of the dogs at bay. It was clear that Josef couldn't keep the pack off him forever, but he was making a go of it.

Behind him, the rabbi was mixing some potion or another, which he tossed at a dog that was edging around Josef's reach. The flask burst on striking the dog's head, splashing a clear liquid all over the dog's snout and head. Any flesh or fur that the liquid touched smoked and melted away, and the dog dropped like a stone within seconds.

The old man and his golem were putting up a hell of a fight, but I knew they'd soon be overrun. I also knew that once I started shooting, the noise would draw deaders and deader dogs from miles around. So, I did the only thing that made sense; I drew my sword and rushed the hounds from behind.

One swipe of my blade resulted in three hounds losing their rear legs. It wouldn't kill them or even stop them, but it would slow them down. Four more were distracted by my attack, and Josef sent them flying with a swing of the light pole. The rabbi threw another flask at the three hounds I'd dropped, and they went up in a blinding flash of green light. I shielded my eyes, and when I looked again there was nothing left of the hounds but ash.

Five left.

Two dogs leapt at me from my right. I swung the sword in a backhand arc, cutting the nose off one and lodging the blade in the other dog's neck. The first dog continued its momentum and hit me full in the chest while the other dog fell, wrenching my blade from my hand. I tumbled over backward with the first dog on top of me.

With no other alternative, I lodged my left forearm in the dog's mouth to prevent it from tearing my throat out. I fumbled for my knife as the dog savaged my arm, and blood flowed freely from my wounds. Suddenly, and without warning, the dog released my arm and backed off me. It began hacking and choking, almost like it was a cat coughing up a fur ball.

Then the damned thing dropped like a brick, and its creepy yellow eyes rolled back in its head. I drew my knife and stabbed it through the skull, just to be sure.

Huh. Proof of concept, I suppose.

I looked up to see that the rabbi and his golem were finishing off the rest of the hounds. Josef ripped the last few into pieces with his massive hands, then stomped their remains into pulp. The rabbi pulled a sword from inside his cane, and he went around cutting the heads off those Josef hadn't seen to yet.

I did a quick check for injuries. My arm was pretty damned torn up, but it could have been much worse. Otherwise, I was fine.

Moments later, the rabbi came back into my line of sight. He leaned over in front of me, using his cane for support as he looked me in the eyes. "Hmph, not a deader yet, I see. This is good!"

"Good to see you too, Rabbi. And in one piece, I might add." I pushed myself to a seated position and wrapped a bandana around my arm, tying it off as I spoke. "What brings you to these parts?"

"I came to warn you that a powerful witch is looking for you."

"Well, she found me. Or rather, I found her. Been planning to take her out, actually. Would you be interested in lending a hand?"

He nodded, and a broad smile split his weathered face. "Pfft, as if I would refuse. When do we start?"

It was comforting to know we'd have the rabbi and Josef on our team when we attempted to pull off my crazy-ass plan. But even with their help and the 'thropes on our side, I still didn't know if we could make it work. The initial attack on Calypso and her brood was crucial, but in the grand scheme of things, all we really needed to do was make sure she was dead.

Without reservation, I was happy to sacrifice myself to make that happen. The plan after that didn't rely on me at all, so even if I died at Calypso's hands it wouldn't matter. Kara knew the rest of the plan, and she'd help the group finish matters in my absence.

Planning for a worst-case scenario was typical bright-side Army Ranger thinking. I'd thought it all through, and calculated the risks. Dying was an acceptable risk, to ensure the future of this group... and potentially the rest of the human race.

But I really hoped it wouldn't come to that.

I got the rabbi back to the Facility and introduced him to the group. He apparently knew Samson from way back, so he and the alpha did some catching up in the mess hall, sharing hilarious war stories with the rest of the group. I was glad to hear some laughter inside the place for a change. My people would need it to face what we were about to do. Many of them wouldn't return, and they all knew it.

I could see it written on their faces, human and 'thrope alike.

My job was to make sure that as many of them as possible made it back from the assault. So, while the rabbi and Samson regaled the group with their tall tales, I got to work. The first step was to ensure that we had an advantage over the vamps. Most were baby vamps and easy enough to kill, but Calypso still had a few mature vamps working for her, and they had me worried. I spent a few hours in the armory working on a surprise for those assholes, then prepped my gear.

After I was ready to roll, I had a quick powwow with the leaders from every group. Gabby and Bobby were there, along with the Doc, Colin, Anna, Mickey, Samson, Sledge, Trina, and the rabbi. I looked across the small gathering and revealed the rest of my plan, as well as Kara's part in it... without mentioning Donnie the Wendigo, of course.

Colin was the first to speak up. "You're fucking crazy, Scratch. Absolutely bugshit nuts. You get within fifty feet of her, and she'll tear you to pieces."

Out of habit, I rubbed my bite scar as I listened to his criticism of my plan. "Don't worry about that. I've got it covered. I'm fairly certain she won't harm me unless she knows that Kara is present. She wants to destroy us both, and make us watch each other die, slowly. She told me as much back at the Reserve Center in Austin."

Bobby cleared his throat to get my attention. "Just how certain is 'fairly certain,' Scratch?"

I shrugged. "Ninety-five percent? Hell, I don't know. I just have a feeling that she wants to make me suffer, and Kara to watch."

Samson tsked softly from the corner of the room. "Yeah, but what happens when she gets wind of Kara?"

I knew that question was coming. "Kara knows how to stay downwind. And besides, she'll be too busy with the battle to notice." *I hope.*

Gabby was twirling and flipping her knife, something she always did when she was nervous. She slammed the butt of the Kabar onto a table, and it was shockingly loud in the small room.

"Just don't get yourself killed, *pendejo*. Or else I'll have my *tia* bring you back to life just so I can kick your ass."

She stormed out of the room. Bobby stood up to follow her, but Samson laid a hand on his shoulder.

"Let her go, son. She just needs some time alone." He looked at me with hooded eyes. "Don't you worry, Scratch. My Pack will do what needs to be done."

I shot the old 'thrope a grim smile. "I appreciate that, Samson. I know y'all could cut and run if you wanted to."

Samson tousled Bobby's hair, and the kid's face split into a sour smile. "Not so long as this knucklehead insists on hanging around with you people. Besides, I'm tired of just surviving. It's time we took our shit back from these bloodsuckers, and made them pay for what they've done." The alpha looked at me. "Speaking of which, you do have a plan for when Calypso's master comes looking for her, don't you?"

I nodded, my face a mask. "Again, I have that covered. But one thing at a time, right? Let's work on taking the witch out, and then we can deal with the rest of the Dallas coven."

Anna looked around the room, then at me. "I'm just not sure I want to lose any more of our boys, Scratch. Can you ensure that you'll keep them safe during the attack?"

I raised both hands in submission. "I make no promises, but we'll keep your Wild Boys and our people outside and in well-lit rooms during the attack. They'll be on fire support duty, helping take out the vamps as Samson and his people lure them out. Since we're attacking during the day, most of her brood should be sound asleep. So, we'll just be contending with her deader dogs and the older vamps."

Mickey shook his head. "I still don't like it."

I shrugged. "It's either this or wait here until they break through Colin's... whatever the hell Colin did to keep them out. Then, we'll be fighting them at night—and you saw how that turned out the last time."

"I could just keep reinforcing my wards," Colin said.

I scratched my head and sighed. "And what if something happens to you? Uh-uh, no way I'm resting our entire defense on one person. Nope. The only solution is to take them out, and the Dallas coven too." I scanned the room, trying to make eye contact with as many of them as I could. "Now, you all know what you have to do. Brief your people, and be ready to roll at oh-six-hundred. Any more questions?"

Bobby raised his hand. "If you die, can I have your room?"

The next morning, we had a crew of some thirty individuals ready to roll out at the designated time. We were leaving a few folks behind, including the Doc because she was too valuable to risk, and all the humans who had refused the serum or tried it with mixed or no results.

Trina was also staying behind, and man, was she pissed about it. But Samson pointed out that she was one of only two trained medical personnel, and that meant we needed to keep her here to run triage and help the Doc treat the wounded after the battle. After a lot of yelling and growling, she finally accepted Samson's orders—although I didn't think she'd ever forgive him for it.

On the plus side, we had two handfuls of 'thropes, an equal number of juiced Wild Boys, and another half-dozen settlers who'd taken to the serum. That was in addition to myself, Bobby, Gabby, Colin, and Anna, who insisted on having the opportunity to die with her people. She was one of the humans who hadn't gotten juiced, so I had mixed emotions about that. But it was ultimately her life and her call, so I let it go.

Besides, Colin said she was a crack shot. Honestly, I didn't mind having someone on overwatch who could shoot the balls off a gnat at a hundred paces. Besides Kara, of course.

Kara wasn't just my ace in the hole; she was the whole plan, period. I assumed that she and Donnie had secreted themselves inside the hospital while the vamps were out attacking us the night previous. I simply had to trust that she'd be in position when the time came.

We pulled up on the hospital at around zero-seven-hundred. While the serum hadn't fully exerted its effects on our humans, the group still moved at a decent clip. Anna hitched a ride on Bobby's back, so we made damned good time. The only thing that slowed us down was killing the sentries we came across on the way. Damned deader dogs were sneaky as all hell. We could've ignored them, since Calypso would know we were coming anyway, but it was the principle of the thing that mattered.

By zero-seven-fifteen we were ready to breach the hospital. All our snipers were in place in key positions around the building, with three-hundred-sixty-degree coverage all around. They'd take out any deaders who were drawn in by the commotion, and if any vamps popped up behind a window on ground level, they were toast.

I prayed that Kara was inside and in position, then signaled to the 'thropes to move out. Gabby was about to follow us in, and I stopped her with a look. "Uh-uh, kiddo, no way in hell. I won't last two seconds in there if I'm worried about looking after you."

She shoved me hard with both hands. "You know what, Scratch? Fuck you! You don't get to decide if I live or die. Tony split, and Lorena is more interested in her Peter dishes than in me, so you're all I have left."

Bobby raised a hand, his brow furrowed in deep thought. "That's 'petri dishes,' I think."

She turned on him and pointed a finger in his face. "You stay out of this, *perro*."

He backed off, hands raised in the air. "Geez, I was just trying to help," he mumbled.

Gabby spun back on me. "So, you're the closest thing to family I have, and there is no way in hell I'm letting you go in there without me. Understood?"

I exhaled heavily, frustrated at the delay. "Nope, no can do. You're not furry enough, and it'll be too easy for one of our snipers to mistake you for a vamp. Besides, I can't do my job while I'm worried about whether or not you're safe." I looked at Bobby. "Keep her outside the building, kid. Or it's your ass when I get back."

Gabby started to say something, then stopped herself and stormed off. Bobby shrugged and went after her, and I watched them go. Samson chuckled and clapped a hand on my shoulder. "I told the boy stay outside as well."

I shook my head. "Has he ever listened to you? They're going to follow us in, just you watch. Let's get in and get out before those two have a chance to get in any real trouble."

I checked my rifle to make sure I had one in the chamber, and switched the selector to full auto. "Now, let's go ruin that bitch's day."

We took off at a sprint toward the hospital. As soon as we hit the parking lot, a wave of undead hounds came flowing out of the hospital straight at us.

We'd prepared for this, and our snipers were already firing by the time we made contact with the hounds. The plan was simple. The snipers would down the deader dogs, and the 'thropes would finish as many of them as possible while I went in with Samson and two more 'thropes. My primary goal was to get to the elevator shaft, where I intended to spring my surprise on Calypso's lieutenants.

And after that? I fully intended to be captured by their master.

The *crack-crack-crack* of rifle fire sounded from all directions as hounds began dropping ahead of us. While the 'thropes couldn't move as fast as vamps, they were still incredibly agile and quick in their full werewolf forms, and they made short work of any hounds that were down. Samson led a spear formation with Sledge and two more wolves with me in the center, and they threw hounds right and left, slashing and tearing as we made our way to the front doors of the hospital.

Finally, we made it inside. Samson posted two 'thropes at the door to keep the deader dogs off our backs, and we entered the interior of the building.

There was plenty of daylight for the first thirty yards or so, but after that I knew it'd be on. My reflexes were a hell of a lot faster now that the deader venom was under control, but if an older vamp showed up I'd still be screwed. I was counting on Calypso ordering them to leave me alone, and it was one hell of a gamble.

I looked at Samson and nodded. "You know what to do. Keep the vamps contained, and keep the kids from heading down the shaft." I shouldered my small ruck and palmed the trigger device in my pocket.

Samson clasped hands with me, his huge werewolf hand enveloping mine. "Good luck, hunter. See you on the other side."

I nodded and sprinted down the hall into the darkness. Shadows were already flitting back and forth in the gloom, and as my eyes adjusted I saw them for what they were: vamps. There were at least three older vamps dashing here and there in the darkness, staying just at the edge of my vision.

And they were so freaking fast. Despite how quick the 'thropes were, and I had no doubt that one of these older vamps would tear the average 'thrope apart in an even fight.

It was my job to give Samson's Pack a fighting chance.

I loosened the straps on my ruck and yelled at the darkness. "Alright, you fuckers, I'm done playing games. Take me to Calypso, now! I've got a deal for her that she can't refuse."

I listened carefully, every sense on high alert. This would all come down to timing, and it was a one-shot deal so I had to make it count. I dropped my rifle to the ground, then took off my katana and laid it next to the rifle. Finally, I unbuckled my belt and let it fall to the floor with my sidearms.

I kicked everything out of reach, then waited to ensure that I knew which direction they were coming from. As I suspected, they approached from behind. Laughter echoed in the darkness, along with the sounds of footsteps that were way to fast and close together, and the *whoosh* of bodies splitting the air at highway speeds.

"Look, I'm unarmed," I said, dropping the backpack to the ground. I raised my hands in the air and took a step forward, waiting for the right moment. *Three sets of footsteps —checkmate.*

A male voice whispered from the darkness behind me.

"Whatever you think you have to offer, your fate is still sealed, human."

"Oh, I'm counting on it," I said as I jumped toward a nearby open doorway, clicking the button on the detonation switch in my pocket as I did.

The explosion in the confined spaces of the hospital hallway was deafening. Inside the pack was a short, pot-shaped steel cylinder, packed with explosives at the base and capped with a concave silver "lid" that I'd had a bitch of a time soldering to the steel casing. This effectively created an explosively-formed penetrator, a type of improvised explosive device that insurgents had used in Iraq and Afghanistan to take out armored vehicles.

The way they worked was simple. When the explosives went off, they super-heated the concave "cap," melting it and forming it into a shaped projectile of molten metal traveling at over a mile a second. Back in the 'Stan I'd seen EFPs penetrate tank armor, so I figured that making one out of molten silver would do a hell of a job on a few vamps. I don't care how scary fast you are; you're still not going to dodge a pound of molten silver flying at 3,600 miles an hour.

As an extra surprise, I'd filled a few waterproof bags with the rest of the scrap silver I had laying around, and packed the ruck with it in front of and around the charge. So, even if the projectile missed one of them, they'd still get a face full of silver for their troubles.

The overpressure from the blast bounced me off a nearby wall, hard enough to leave a large indent in the drywall. *Thank God for cheap modern construction and weak walls,* I thought. I was covered in drywall dust and my ears were ringing like mad, but I was still alive and no vamps were chomping on my face. I counted that as a win.

I rolled over and peeked around the corner. The air was still filled with dust and haze, but it was clear that at least one of the damned things had been hit. It was lying on the ground, rolling back and forth and moaning as thick dark blood flowed from the stumps where its legs had once been.

As the haze cleared, it revealed another injured vamp farther down the hall. Its flesh sizzled and bubbled in numerous places where dozens of makeshift silver projectiles had hit it. I stumbled into the hall and found my sword, drawing it and letting the scabbard fall to the floor. I staggered to the nearest vamp, the one with no legs, and sliced its head off. I did the same to the other one while it was still stunned, and watched its head roll away with disinterest.

But where is the third vamp? My question was answered when a pale white blur knocked my sword from my hands. The vamp grabbed me by the throat with one hand, lifting me off the ground just as Calypso herself had done recently. I struggled against its grip, but my neck may as well have been caught in a bear trap. No matter how much I squirmed, I was not getting free.

"To hell with my mistress' wishes, hunter. I'm going to bleed you dry, here and now, and tell her I had to do it."

I choked out my reply as I felt myself fading out. "Might... want... to rethink that," I said, just as Samson's clawed hand emerged from the vamp's chest. Shock and disbelief registered on the vamp's face as he released me, and I fell to the floor. I looked up just in time to see the old 'thrope pull his arm free, right before he took the vamp's head off with one swipe.

Samson grinned and offered me a hand. "Thing about us 'thropes... we're pretty damned stealthy when we need to be."

"Thanks for the assist," I wheezed, grabbing the furry hand that dripped with thick black blood. I allowed the alpha to pull me to my feet, and leaned against the wall for support.

"Don't mention it. Can you do what needs to be done?"

I struggled to my feet and nodded. "Pretty sure she's waiting for me down that shaft. You'd best be going."

"Don't have to tell me twice. I like you, but not enough to die for you. I didn't get this old by being stupid." The alpha turned and loped toward the exit. "Good luck, hunter," he said over his shoulder as he sprinted off down the hall.

"Thanks," I muttered. "I'm going to need it."

DREAMING

I was banged up pretty good, my balance and hearing were shot from the blast, and after getting choked by that vamp I damned sure wouldn't be singing any showtunes for the next several days, but I was alive.

Yeah, but for how long? I wondered. I put that thought aside, because the only thing that mattered was ensuring the survival of the group. Gabby, Bobby, the Doc, the settlers, the LARPers... hell, taking out the Dallas coven might even secure a future for an untold number of human survivors. And that started here, by ending Calypso.

I gathered what was left of my gear, which included my sword and my pistol belt. Strapping them on, I staggered toward the elevator shaft.

Climbing down was a pain in the ass, what with the equilibrium issues I was having. My ears weren't leaking fluid, but being in close proximity to the IED had really done a number on me. I made it down the elevator shaft by hooking my arms over each step, hanging on for dear life as I slowly lowered myself down. When I got to the bottom, I looked up at the dim light coming in from the open elevator doors above, and everything started to spin. I fell to my knees and wretched up what little I'd had for breakfast, all over a deader dog corpse.

Calypso's voice echoed from the darkness. "You're in no condition to attack, so I assume you're here to parley." I looked up and saw her shadow in the gloom of the tunnel. She cocked her head and tsked. "You've killed my offspring—a shame. They'd been with me for more than a century. But I can always make more."

She remained hidden in the shadow of the tunnel, back where a rifle round couldn't reach her. I needed to draw her out in the center of the shaft, where Kara could take her shot. Another wave of nausea had filled my mouth with saliva, so I spat on the corpses beneath me, then rolled over to sit against the concrete elevator shaft.

"You don't seem to be too upset with me about killing your children."

She stood still as a statue in the darkness, but her voice carried the weight of her indifference. "As I said, I can make more. My kind don't tend to be very sentimental about our offspring. They are somewhat expendable."

"Yet it seems you took the death of your brother very, very hard indeed."

She stared at me in the darkness, silent. "You taunt me, perhaps hoping for a quick death. Your time will come soon enough."

I whispered almost inaudibly, knowing she'd be able to hear. "I did come to strike a bargain, Calypso. I can give you Kara. She's the one who killed your brother. I'd have been happy to have left him in peace."

"Pfah. You lie. I've searched for her since my brother passed, and yet she's eluded me at every step."

"I've seen her—recently, in fact. Take a sniff, and tell me if your senses deceive you."

She inhaled deeply and slowly, like a sommelier taking in the bouquet of a fine wine. "You've been near one of Piotr's brood. You speak the truth."

"I do. She came to me at night, and told me she'd been watching over me," I whispered. "She says she's tired of her unlife, and ready to end it to save me."

"So, she's here," the ancient vampire hissed. "How *interesting*. And she wishes to trade her life for yours?"

Kara dropped to the bottom of the elevator shaft next to me. "I do."

What the hell? This wasn't the plan.

Calypso's laugh was filled with bitterness and hate. "You'll watch him die, and there's nothing you can do about it."

She whirred across the space between them, snatching up a hooked piece of rebar and stabbing Kara through the chest, pinning her to the wall. It was done so fast that if I hadn't had an enhanced perception speed, I would have missed it. One second she was standing in the tunnel, and the next Kara was hanging by that piece of steel.

It was all I could do to stand there, stunned by this turn of events. For one, I didn't think it was possible to stab a length of rebar into reinforced concrete. Second, I couldn't for the life of me figure out why Kara had dropped into the elevator shaft with me. She was supposed to be high above us with that Barrett fifty-cal, waiting to send Calypso back where she belonged. And third, I didn't see how I could hope to turn things around, considering how unbelievably fast Calypso moved. Even with my enhanced reflexes, there was no way I could match her speed.

But maybe, just maybe, there was a chance in hell to salvage this thing.

"Go ahead then, bitch. End it," I whispered, before I

screamed at the top of my lungs, a hate-filled roar that came from the hidden and primal depths of my being. "End it, damn it!"

Calypso regarded Kara as she wriggled and squirmed in agony, like a bug pinned to the ground by a cruel child. She ran her fingers lazily across the sword handle, then turned her eyes on me.

"I intend to, hunter. But not quickly, or easily. No, I will drain you slowly and painfully from a thousand cuts, licking your life from you a drop at a time. All the while, your beloved will watch helplessly, then she'll bear witness while I raise you from the dead as a ghoul to do my bidding." She smiled, baring her fangs. "And then I'll kill her as well."

Calypso was on me in a fraction of a second, barely the time it might take to twitch an eye. She grabbed me by the upper arms so I couldn't struggle, and snapped her head forward so her lips were against the bare skin of my neck. She took another long sniff, and her cold dead breath chilled my flesh as she spoke.

"Mmmm, yes... You smell different today, hunter. The scent of death no longer lingers within you. Let us see how you taste, hmmm?"

She sank her teeth into the side of my neck and blood flowed freely, hot and wet down my shoulder and chest. Calypso drank greedily from me, then clapped a hand over the wound to staunch the blood flow. Even so, I was already getting woozy from blood loss.

"Delicious, but I mustn't end your life too soon, eh? I want to savor the sensation of feeling your life drain from you slowly, bit by bit. Then, I'll..."

The vampire stopped mid-sentence, and her face contorted in pain. "Something's not right—your blood, it's tainted!"

Calypso dropped me to the ground, and blood began flowing from my neck again, soaking my shirt in a spreading dark stain. "They're called antibodies, bitch. How do you think I survived a deader bite without getting turned? All those centuries on earth, and you still skipped science class. Sucks for you," I whispered.

Blood continued to flow from my wound, and now it was staining the ground beneath me. I tried clamping a hand over it to stop the bleeding, or to at least slow it down, but she'd bitten me deep.

Yup, you're going to bite the bullet on this one, I thought. *May as well make it count.* I reached down for my sidearm, fumbling the draw with my slick, bloody fingers. Calypso had staggered against the wall opposite me, but I still thought I could get a clean head shot... if I didn't pass out first.

The witch looked at me with hatred in her eyes. "I'll still kill you," she rasped, "before I die. I swear it."

I managed to get the gun in my hand, just as she was pushing herself off the wall. Her skin and mouth were smoldering now, everywhere my blood touched her. Although it was clear that she'd been badly compromised by the antibodies in my blood, she was determined to end my existence. She lurched toward me, closing the distance between us step by agonizing step.

Nausea and blood loss were doing a job on me, and my vision was fading. I tried to steady the barrel of the gun, but it kept moving around on me. Or maybe Calypso's head was moving around on me—I couldn't be certain. I fired once, and the round pinged off the wall. Again, I squeezed the trigger, and I missed. Then a third time, and a fourth, but I barely managed to graze her shoulder. I emptied the magazine at her, and my rounds hit everywhere but where it counted.

Then she was standing over me, and I was pulling the trigger on an empty chamber, with the slide locked back. She batted the gun away, almost drunkenly, and grabbed me by the neck with both hands. As she lifted me off the ground, I smiled.

"I won," I whispered.

"But I have the last laugh," she rasped.

She began to squeeze, and I felt the vertebrae and connective tissue in my neck shift and pop. Blackness began to close in from the periphery of my vision, until all I saw was the smoldering wreck that was left of her mouth, split into a leer that said I'd triumphed, but at great cost.

Then, her head exploded as the boom of a large-bore rifle echoed in the confines of the elevator shaft. Calypso's body collapsed, and mine with it. I fell in a heap next to her headless corpse, and slowly craned my head to look at where Kara had been pinned to the wall just moments before.

But in her place now was Donnie, stabbed through the chest by that length of rebar. He stood there examining his filthy, raptor-like nails, as if he hadn't a care in the world.

"Hey there, Scratch... would it hurt your feelings if I told you you're not looking so good?"

Kara landed lightly at the bottom of the shaft, dropping the Barrett as she knelt beside me. She tore open a nylon carrier pouch on her belt and pulled out a green plastic packet. She ripped that open to reveal a pressure dressing, which she applied to the wound on my neck.

"Careful... with my blood."

"Ssshh, I'll be fine. This gauze contains a wound-clotting agent. It should stop the bleeding."

"Hell of a switch you two pulled," I murmured. "Could have told me beforehand, you know."

She shook her head. "Your reactions needed to be real.

Calypso knew you were trying to deceive her; vampires are supernatural lie detectors. We can smell the hormones your body releases, hear your heartbeat, and see when your breath rate increases. Sorry, but I had to keep you in the dark to make this work."

"Why'd it take you so long to take the shot?" I asked.

"I had to make it count, so I waited to make sure she was mostly incapacitated before I pulled the trigger."

"Well, I can't argue with your logic. But next time, I get to pull the trigger, and you get to be the one getting their neck snapped."

She leaned over and kissed me on the forehead. "Like you'd ever let that happen."

It took me a few days to heal up from the punishment I'd received at the hands of the vamps... and my own cockamamie schemes. Fortunately, my body was healing a hell of a lot faster now that the Doc's vaccine had helped my system fight off the deader venom.

As for the group, casualties had been minimal—mostly because everyone had stuck to the plan during the attack. Gabby and Bobby had tried to follow me in, just as I'd predicted, but Samson had caught them and nipped that in the bud. Once the fight was over, the wolves pulled me out of the shaft, and then they killed every sleeping vampire they found.

All except one, that is. We let that one live, although we made it look like an oversight. Why? Because we needed to make sure the Dallas coven knew where to find us.

"How long you think it'll take her to get back to Dallas?" I asked Kara. She was sitting in a chair next to me, in a room on the lab level of the Facility. I didn't think the group would be keen on the idea of having a vamp underground with us, so I'd had the Doc sneak her in.

"On foot? A week, at least. Less, if she manages to hijack a vehicle."

"Unlikely. We found where Calypso had hidden her trucks, and tucked them away on the base where no one is going to find them." I stroked the five-day beard on my chin. "Still, it doesn't give us much time to do what needs to be done. Did you sift through the intel we recovered?"

"I did, with the Doc's help. The codes were there, although it remains to be seen whether or not they'll get us in."

I yawned. "We'll take the rabbi and Josef with us, just in case. If we can't get in the place through conventional means, Josef can just bust his way through. Either that, or we can dig our way in with heavy equipment, with all the diesel we found in the back of their trucks."

"You think it'll work?" she asked.

"It has to. This is the only way I can think of to take those dickheads out in one fell swoop. We have to end it, Kara."

"And we will, Scratch. We will. I just..."

I took her hands in mine. They were cold, and way too unyielding for human flesh, but I didn't care. After everything that had happened, I'd realized that deep down inside she was the same Kara I'd always known.

"You're wondering what happens after, right?"

She nodded.

"I'm sticking with you, Kara, to the bitter end. Maybe we find a cure for your... condition. Or maybe we just do like I said and live happily ever after. I still have the ranch, and it's secluded enough that we could hide out there indefinitely."

"And when humans come for me? What will you do then?"

"You still have your humanity intact, Kara. You're different now, but you're still you."

"I'm me, Scratch, but I'm not human anymore—not by any stretch. And if there was a cure for vampirism, the Doc would have told you by now."

I squeezed her hands. "Trust me, we can make it work. But first, we just have to finish this one last thing. I can't leave them until I know they're going to be alright."

"To the bitter end, then," she said, smiling and inadvertently revealing her too-long canines.

"You can bank on it. I'm not going anywhere, unless it means following you."

A cough from outside the door told me the Doc wanted to speak to us, but she didn't want to intrude.

"Come on in, Doc."

The Doc opened the door and entered the room, shutting it behind her even though no one was likely to be within listening range... except for Gabby, of course. But the Doc wouldn't have been here to discuss matters unless her niece was busy elsewhere.

"I take it Gabby is busy preparing, along with everyone else?" I asked.

The Doc nodded. "Everything seems to be going as planned. We're pumping ground water into the long-term storage tanks, to ensure they're full of clean water. We've sent out two-person teams to hunt for game, and we've organized a kitchen crew to preserve the meat. Others are scavenging in the northern part of the city and on base for canned goods, and we have teams looking for fresh produce at farms to the west and north."

"Did anyone contact Margie and Bernie?"

She pursed her lips. "Yes, but we had a hard time getting them to come. Gabby and Bobby finally convinced them it was in their best interests."

I breathed a sigh of relief. "Well, that's some good news. How about the preparations at the old hospital?"

"We formed a detail made up of 'thropes and humans, and they're working to make it look like we're using it for our base now. Within a few days, it'll look like we're living there."

I closed my eyes, bringing up the rest of my to-do list from memory. "And the entrances to the Facility are all well-hidden?"

She nodded. "All except for the ones we'll need to access when we make our escape."

I pulled myself up higher in the bed, using my elbows for support. "Alright then." I rubbed my hands together and gave them my best shit-eating grin. "Let's go steal ourselves a nuclear warhead."

TIME

THE TRIP to Amarillo was mostly uneventful. Our group consisted of myself, Kara, the two knuckleheads, the rabbi and his golem, and Sledge. Colin stayed behind, just in case more vamps showed up. He was sore about it, but I felt better about having him and the Pack looking after everyone. Everyone who was left, that was.

We drove at night—or rather, Kara drove at night—in blackout mode, to avoid drawing much attention from humans who might want to get their own working military transport truck to drive around. The damned thing was loud as hell, so it attracted deaders like the dickens, but Kara sent out her vampire radar signal, and that mostly kept them away. The biggest issue we had was making it through pile-ups, but between Josef, Bobby, and Sledge, we were able to clear each roadblock without a hassle.

I rode with Kara in the cab, since no one else seemed comfortable riding shotgun with her. Besides, I'd missed her company. We'd lived together on and off for years, but hell if I didn't realize how much I needed her 'til she was gone. We spoke at length regarding what she'd been doing since we'd parted ways in Austin, what it was like to be a vampire, and the career she'd had as a nuclear physicist before the War. It was enlightening, to say the least.

As it turned out, we still had a lot more in common than I would have guessed.

The trip was long—an eight-hour drive on clear roads at highway speeds before the War—and it gave us plenty of time to catch up along the way. We spent the first day resting at an abandoned farm near the halfway point outside of Flat Top, Texas. The scene around the farm indicated that a huge roving herd of deaders had been through recently, killing everything in sight. The farmhouse had nearly been pushed off its foundations by the deader swarm, and vegetation had been trampled in a half-mile wide swath that traversed the countryside as far as the eye could see.

Inside the house, there was gore everywhere. From what I could tell, none of the inhabitants had survived being bitten, since they'd been ripped to shreds. Small comfort, that—but at least the poor folks weren't sentenced to decades of roaming the plains of Texas until their legs wore down to nubs.

The downside was that the house was a wreck, and unsafe to boot. So, we pulled the truck in the metal barn, which was still mostly intact, and set a watch to make sure no one snuck up on us while we let Kara sleep. The rest of us slept in shifts, and outside of the odd deader, we rested undisturbed. That evening, we loaded up and continued our trek north.

It wasn't until we got close to Panhandle, just northeast of Amarillo, when Kara alerted me to the bad news. She pulled to a stop at around 4:00 a.m. or so, on a highway rise where we had a clear view of the land ahead. In the dark under starlight and moonlight, her vision was as sharp as mine was in daytime, so she was the first to spot them.

Kara turned off the engine and tapped me on the arm. "Scratch, look."

She pointed over the dash and off to the horizon. I couldn't see much, despite having pseudo-werewolf vision from the Doc's serum. The changes allowed me to see in very low-light conditions, but they did nothing to enhance my ability to see at a distance.

"I don't see anything. What is it, punters? Another damned road block?"

"No, nothing that simple. Listen."

I listened, and soon realized our predicament. Their moans were a low roar in the night, background noise that had blended with the clatter of the truck's diesel engine. I was only noticing it now because the engine was silent, save for a few clicks and pings from it slowly cooling down in the night air.

I pulled out a pair of binoculars and opened the door of the truck, stepping out and climbing up on the hood to get a good luck.

"Holy mother of mercy," I growled. "That's a shit-ton of deaders."

The rabbi, Gabby, and Bobby had awoken and crawled out of the back of the truck to see what was up. Gabby whistled softly. "*Híjole*, but that's an understatement. I've never seen so many deaders in one place."

Sledge walked up beside the hood, so I knelt down and handed him the binoculars. He surveyed the huge mass of deaders and shook his head. "Damn, Scratch. Looks like we came all the way out here for nothing."

The huge 'thrope offered the binoculars to the rabbi, who declined them. "I can't see what's out there, but I have ears to hear." He looked up at me with a resigned expression. "Hunter, unless you want to let the dead ones have your *kishkes* for breakfast, I'd say we're through here."

I took the binocs back from Sledge and scanned the land ahead of us. Deaders milled about in a loose formation over four square miles or more, covering what must have once been the Pantex plant. I had no idea how many deaders it might take to cover that much land, but it had to be in the millions.

Kara hopped out of the truck and sat on the hood next to me. "They're right, Scratch. This mission is a bust. Let's head back and find someplace to hide out overnight—someplace far away from the world's largest mosh pit up ahead."

I continued to scan the area, doing my best to make out landmarks in the sea of bodies. The intel we'd recovered from Calypso had included aerial photos of the plant, and before we'd left I'd studied them until I had them memorized. Our plan had been to reach the plant and then access two key areas: the disassembly facilities inside the plant, and a temporary underground storage facility where they kept weapons-grade plutonium before converting it to its less dangerous plutonium oxide form.

We were looking for a W-76 nuclear warhead, and enough weapons grade plutonium-239 to get the yield we needed. That was my big plan for taking out the Dallas coven, and now I had umpteen million deaders standing between me and my swan song. I kept sweeping the binoculars left and right, marking entrances and exit points, escape routes, and distances in my head.

"We could draw them off," Bobby suggested. "Maybe with an explosion or something. Heck, we have all this diesel in the back of the truck. I'm pretty sure we could find some fertilizer to mix with it—we are in the middle of farm country, after all. We'd just need to fix up a bomb, detonate it wherever we wanted the herd to go, and then we could get in while they were out taking a hike."

"Wouldn't work," Gabby replied. "That herd is too damned big. You might pull off a fourth or half of them, but the rest would just get agitated and scatter like a scared flock of birds. No telling where they'd run if that happened. Anyone within a mile of that place would be trampled within minutes."

I grunted my approval as I lowered the binoculars. "It's a damned good plan, Bobby, but Gabby's right. Besides, I have a better idea."

Kara squeezed her eyes shut and began rubbing her temples. "I knew you were going to suggest this," she muttered.

"Suggest what?" Sledge asked.

Gabby crossed her arms and scowled at me as she answered Sledge's question. "You only haven't figured it out because you haven't been around this *pendejo loco* very long. Scratch is planning to head in on foot, because he thinks he's the zombie whisperer."

We'd withdrawn to a safer position a few miles south of the plant, hiding out in an abandoned grain and feed store in the tiny town of Washburn. The whole place was deserted—what little of it there was, anyway. I doubted there'd been many people living there before the dead came, but now it truly was a ghost town. I wondered what had happened to these folks, and all those people in Amarillo, just up the road. Perhaps many of them were now camped out at Pantex with the rest of the dead.

Kara had slipped off to a dark, quiet place under the floorboards of the building, leaving the rest of us to argue over the best course of action—which we did for most of the morning. Finally, everyone realized we were getting nowhere, so we each retreated to separate parts of the building to sleep. Now, it was getting close to sundown, and everyone was sulking around inside the feed store and pointedly avoiding talking with me.

All except for the rabbi, of course. He knew what was at stake, because the old man had been around a few times. I had a feeling he'd witnessed more than one holocaust in his day, and he was all for ending this one.

"You think she can do it?" he said in hushed tones.

"Yes, I believe she can. But you don't have to come along, Rabbi. Kara and I can handle this on our own."

He shook his head and gave me a stern look. "Bah! What if you can't get in? She is strong, yes—but not as strong as Josef, *ja*? And while I could send him along without me, I'm unable to exert control over him at great distances. I can give him simple commands, of course, but without me to guide him he might misinterpret them and smash into the wrong building, or cause some other catastrophe. No, it is settled. I will come with you."

"Fine, but if something goes wrong, you hop on Josef's shoulders and get the hell out of there, alright?"

"*Ja, ja,* I have been hunting much longer than you. I know how to stay alive."

"So, we're doing it?" I turned, slightly startled, to see Kara standing next to me. She'd appeared soundlessly and out of nowhere. It was going to take some getting used to, this being in love with a vampire thing.

"It appears we are. Did you rest well?" I asked.

"I did, but I'm going to need to feed soon."

The rabbi held up his hands in protest. "Don't look at me! I'm a tolerant individual when it comes to benevolent supernatural creatures, but my magnanimity has its limits."

Kara chuckled softly. "Don't worry, Rabbi, I'm not hungry enough to lose control. Yet."

She said that last part with a glimmer in her eye, and her

voice deepened slightly. It was all I could do to keep from drawing down on her. *Yeah, this is definitely going to take getting used to.*

"Well, we'd better get going then," I said. "Hopefully we can get in and out before midnight, so Kara can have time to hunt."

I walked over to the rest of our small party to give them their final instructions. "We're going to be heading out in a few—me, Kara, the rabbi, and the golem."

Gabby wouldn't meet my gaze. "You're going to get yourself killed," she mumbled.

Bobby frowned. "I was going to say, 'Don't get yourself killed.' Thanks for stealing my line, Gabby."

She elbowed him in the shoulder, putting some steam on it, and Bobby tumbled off his chair. "Damn it, *perro*, this is no time for jokes!" She stood suddenly, fists clenched, eyes narrowed, staring at my shoes.

"Gabby, it's going to be alright," I said softly.

She closed the distance in two quick strides and pulled me into a bear hug, her face against my chest. It was a surprising display of affection from the girl, and much like her uncle I wasn't good at this sort of thing. Still, I reached up and hugged her around the shoulders, patting her back as she sobbed into my chest.

"Ssshh, it's okay. I'll be fine—deaders don't like the taste of me, remember? Besides, Kara and the rabbi will be there watching my back."

"But what if something happens? What if you don't come back? We won't be able to come after you, and..." She broke off mid-sentence, unable to complete that thought.

I gently peeled her off me and took a half-step back, reaching up to lift her chin with one hand. "Listen, kid—I'd never abandon you, alright? You gotta believe me on this. I fully intend to get in, get out, and make it back to you two knuckle-heads. Have a little faith, hmm? I've made it out of worse than this."

She smiled sadly and shook her head. *"Estás siendo tonto—* you've never faced down millions of deaders."

"Yeah, maybe not, but I've walked right through herds of them before, and they ignored me. There's no reason to think that these deaders will act any different. And Kara's going to do her vampire mind-control thing to keep them away from us. So, cheer up, alright? I'll be back before you know it."

She wiped her eyes with her sleeve. "Okay, but get back fast."

Bobby sniffled nearby. "Aw, man, what a breakthrough for you two. Wait 'til I tell the Doc about how you bonded over the prospects of Scratch's imminent death."

Gabby spun and punched him in the arm. "Not a word of this, to anyone!" She punched him again, harder. "And stop saying stuff like that before you jinx him, *payaso.*"

He grabbed his shoulder and shied away. "Okay, geez." The kid turned to me and stuck out his hand. "Good luck, Scratch. Come back safe, alright?"

"I will, kid. I promise."

<hr />

"You have a habit of making promises you know you can't keep," Kara said as we jogged alongside the huge flesh golem. The rabbi rode on his shoulders, hopefully out of reach of any curious deaders. We'd slathered ourselves in deader guts before heading out, and I hoped between that, the lingering deader venom in my veins, Kara's vampire mojo, and the undead state of the golem, we'd be able to get in and back out again unmolested.

I tsked as I glanced her way. "I keep my promises, as best I can."

"Yes, but you're always promising the impossible. It's a bad habit, Scratch. You set expectations way too high for your own accomplishments, especially when others are depending on you. It leaves you vulnerable to looking like an ass when you let them down."

I looked up at the rabbi. "You ever been in love, Borovitz?"

"Oh no, don't drag me into your *mishegoss*."

Kara snorted, her eyes twinkling. "Looks like you're on your own, Scratch. The rabbi knows better than to stick his nose where it's not welcomed."

"Thanks a lot, Rabbi."

He lifted his hands up as he shrugged. "What do you want me to say? You dig a pit and fall in, it's up to you to get yourself out."

We came to a small rise, and Kara slowed her pace as she held a finger to her lips. "Ssshh, I think we're getting close to the edge of the mob. Stay close and keep quiet until we know it's working."

"You set the pace, we'll follow," I said.

"Here goes nothing," she replied, and began walking over the hill.

As we crested the rise, a sea of dead spread out before us. The moaning was fairly loud, but not overwhelming since the dead were fairly sparse in this area. But just a few hundred yards ahead, they stood nearly shoulder to shoulder.

Shit, one wrong move and we'll be trampled, I thought. I held my breath as Kara strolled forward, waiting to see if the deaders would react to the signal she was trying to send out to them.

We were fifty feet away, then forty, then thirty. Still, nothing happened. Although we were moving silently, a few of the outliers noticed us, and they began to moan louder as they shuffled our direction.

I froze, as did the rabbi and Josef, but Kara continued on. When she got maybe ten feet from the approaching deaders, they stopped in their tracks, looking confused and unsure of what to do. Finally, they backed off and a small bubble of empty space opened around her as she strolled ahead. I looked at the rabbi, and he returned my glance. We gave a collective sigh and hurried after her.

Progress was slow from there on. As the crowd grew denser, it took longer for the dead to shamble away from us. Every so often, one or two would approach us instead of yielding the right of way, and Kara would pause. I assumed she was exerting more pressure, or boosting her signal, or whatever vamps did to keep the dead at bay. In these cases, the dead would lose interest after a few moments, and we'd continue on.

The noise was deafening. Not just the moans, but the clacking of teeth, the *skritch-skritch-skritch* of bone rubbing on bone, the sounds of millions of feet scraping the ground as the dead shuffled back and forth, back and forth, in a hypnotic and never-ending dance. I cut a few pieces of cloth from my shirttail and shoved them in my ears.

Soon, I was lost in my own thoughts, trying very hard to avoid freaking out due to the sounds, the overpowering reek of rotting flesh, and the ever-present press of the dead around us. My movements became rhythmic after a time, as I did my best to imitate the plodding pace at which I'd seen so many deaders march.

Lost in my head, I nearly bumped into Kara as she came to a halt. She signaled for me to stand next to her, and she leaned in close, placing her lips next to my ears.

"Something isn't right."

I leaned back and raised an eyebrow.

"I don't know," she whispered. "I sense something else is out here with us."

I didn't know what else to do, so I motioned for her to keep going. Just as she was taking a step forward, the rabbi tapped me on the shoulder. Kara paused, and we followed the rabbi's gaze as he slowly lifted his arm and pointed at our one o'clock.

Something was causing a stir in the herd ahead, maybe a hundred yards distant. The dead were parting there as well, and whatever was causing the commotion was headed our way.

I looked at Kara, and she mouthed one word.

Vamps.

OFFICE

We were just steps away from one of the disassembly facilities, so I motioned that we should get moving and avoid an altercation, if possible. We forged ahead and approached a side entrance to one of the many warehouse-like buildings on the site. The place had been locked down tight before the War, that much was clear. While the security fences around the facility had all been torn down, the heavy metal doors preventing access to the building were intact.

We hadn't expected the power to be on, so we knew we couldn't just swipe a keycard to get inside. However, we'd also come prepared with lockpicks as well as a fully-charged car battery and a DC to AC inverter to power the electronic locks on the doors. Hopefully, they'd still open after all this time.

We crouched nervously near the entrance, hiding from any passersby among the sea of dead shuffling about. Kara must have eased off her anti-deader signal, because the mass of zombies pressed in against us, ignoring us but shuffling way too close for comfort. *At least we're somewhat hidden,* I thought.

It was clear that someone was moving through the throng of shamblers. They had to be vamps, because the dead moved away from them like Moses parting the waters. That much we could see, even from our low vantage point. As they passed, by no one spoke or even twitched a muscle. I was pretty sure the rabbi was holding his breath—I know I was.

It took a minute or so, but soon the disturbance in the crowd of dead passed us by. I took a deep, gasping breath.

"That was close," I whispered. "Who do you think it was?"

Kara looked worried. "No idea, but from what I could tell they were young vamps. Older vamps use the younger ones for their grunt work, running patrols and security. So, it's likely there are older vamps around that are just as dangerous as Piotr and Calypso."

"Shit," I replied. "Alright, so we're not alone. That still doesn't change the plan. Let's get inside, grab what we need, and get the hell out of here."

I started messing with the keypad beside the door, intending to expose the wiring beneath, but the rabbi stopped me with a hand on my arm. He grabbed the door handle and depressed the release, and the door cracked open with a squeal of rusted metal.

I looked at the rabbi and Kara. "Looks like the Coven isn't worried about anyone breaking in."

Kara frowned. "Not with all these deaders around. Should work in our favor, though, since they obviously aren't expecting guests."

The old man dug around in his bag and pulled out a small plastic bottle. "Silicone lubricant," he replied. "Odorless. Comes in handy when you're sneaking around after the apocalypse, *ja*?" He dabbed a bit on each hinge and wiped off the excess. We waited for a few moments, then the rabbi opened the door. "After you," he said, with a slight bow to Kara.

We ducked inside, weapons at the ready, but we were alone. According to our intel, this was where nuclear warheads had been disassembled during decommissioning, once the radioactive elements had been removed. I looked around the place; it was like stepping into a time capsule. Except for a few footprints in the dust that were way too far apart, the place had been left untouched. The footprints indicated that vamps had passed through here, but they'd decided that what they needed was elsewhere in the plant.

Lucky for us, this had also been where decommissioned weapons were updated and put back into service. According to the information we'd stolen from Calypso, the plant had gone into high gear reassembling warheads after the first bombs fell. By some miracle, the place hadn't been hit by a nuclear bomb, probably because the vamps had wanted to keep it intact.

Or, they simply hadn't known about it. Either way, it was just dumb luck that the place hadn't been flattened. I was fairly positive that the storage facilities here were designed to survive a direct hit, but the manufacturing and assembly areas probably wouldn't have made it. Since we needed the tools and equipment in those labs to put together a working nuclear weapon, I counted my blessings that the place hadn't been breached.

Strange that the dead haven't gotten in, though, I thought. "Kara, what are the odds that the vamps are using that horde of dead outside for security—you know, to keep humans away from here?"

She tapped a finger on her chin as she considered my question. "Now that you mention it, it does seem a little odd that they're just standing around. Why would they march all the way across the state, just to get here and stop? None of it makes sense, at least not without vamps being behind it."

The rabbi tsked. "So, they were herded here for a purpose."

I thought back to the farmhouse where we'd stayed on the trip north. Based on what I'd seen inside, the dead had been through there fairly recently, maybe in the last few weeks.

I smacked my forehead in frustration. "Damn it! It's so obvious, I never even considered it. They've been here recovering plutonium for weeks. Calypso never needed to get that intel back to Dallas, because she was in contact with them the whole time via her connection to her master. Hell, her mission might have been to distract us and keep us pinned down, just to make sure we didn't interfere with their recovery operations. Man, but I feel like an idiot!"

"*Ja jaeger*, but none of us saw this coming. Don't beat yourself up too badly for not being clairvoyant."

Kara laid a hand on my arm. "Hang on a minute, Scratch... what if this works in our favor?"

"How so?"

"Well, what if they came out in force to make this happen? What if the Dallas coven is here? Then, we don't have to get them to come to us. All we need to do is set the trap and get the hell out of here without tipping our hand."

I looked at the rabbi, and he nodded as he rubbed his chin. "She has a point. It could work."

I grabbed both sides of Kara's face and gave her an enthusiastic kiss. "Baby, you're a genius." Her lips were cold and unnaturally firm, but they responded in kind so I didn't care.

She smiled slightly as I pulled away from her. "FYI, this genius has always hated it when you called me baby," she said softly. "But I'll let it slide this once."

"So, what is our plan?" the rabbi asked.

I tapped a finger on my chin as I gathered my thoughts. "Kara, what's the blast radius of a W-76 warhead?"

She scrunched her forehead and squinted one eye shut as she ran the calculations in her head. "A hundred megaton yield is standard for that warhead. I'd say the kill zone would be three miles, give or take. But considering the usual weather patterns out here, the fallout will be following us back to Austin. We'll need to evacuate in a different direction, or be long gone when the device detonates."

And if Bobby, Gabby, and Sledge were still in that feed store when the thing went off... I just didn't want to think about it.

"Alright, that gives me something to work with. Kara, you take Josef and the rabbi to get what you need to cook us up a working nuclear warhead. It doesn't look like there are any deaders inside the plant, so I'm going to scout around and make sure that the Dallas coven is really here."

Kara crossed her arms and shook her head. "Nope, it'll take you too long and you're more likely to get caught. Tell you what, I'll do the scouting while you and the rabbi take Lurch here to snag some plutonium. Chances are good that I'll already have the device ready by the time you come back. And if the Dallas coven is here, then we blow them to hell. If not, we take the device back and get them to come to us, then we blow them to hell. Deal?"

"Fine, fine—be all liberated and stuff, see if I care," I said with a halfhearted frown. "Just please be safe."

"I believe that goes without saying, but I appreciate that you're so concerned about my welfare. Now get moving, because as slow as you two are, I'll likely be done by the time you get back."

"Whatever," I said with a slight smile. "Rabbi, you ready?"

"Of course. Let us be on our way."

I headed down the hall, but was stopped by a red-haired, pale-skinned blur. Kara pecked me on the cheek, then she stepped aside.

"Now you can go," she said, before effectively disappearing from our view by moving at top vampire speed.

204 / M.D. MASSEY

The rabbi chuckled and gave me a wink. "She is quite the woman, *ja*? More than a match for you, I think."

I began walking down the hall, senses on high alert. "You think we can make it work?"

He shrugged. "Anything is possible. You love each other, so that is in your favor. I've seen many interspecies relationships in my time, between supernatural creatures and humans. Some worked out, and some ended in tragedy. You simply cannot know the outcome of such a union until you try." He paused and glanced at me sideways. "And you're not exactly human anymore, yourself."

"I suppose that's true, Rabbi. I guess now that I know she's still the same Kara deep down, all the rest doesn't matter. I thought I'd lost her once, when the 'thropes took her, and again when I discovered she was a vamp. At this point getting her back, or even the prospect of it—well, let's just say I'm not one to look a gift horse in the mouth."

"And you'd do well not to—" he cut himself off, continuing in hushed tones. "Josef senses someone coming. We must hide, now!"

A quick scan of the area revealed no readily available place of concealment. I looked at the floor behind us, groaning inwardly at the tracks in the dust that we'd left.

"I don't think that's an option, Rabbi," I whispered as I drew my katana and went back to back with Josef, who picked the rabbi up and placed him on his shoulders.

"I smell human blood," a male voice whispered. He had a strong Gulf coast accent, so I knew he wasn't a local. He chuckled softly, then his laughter faded into a low growl. "And I hear two heartbeats."

"Be ready, *jaeger*," the rabbi whispered, although for what I had no idea. I tightened my grip on my sword.

A tall, slender man with dirty blond hair flitted into view

ahead of us, dressed in faded jeans, All-Stars, and a Kanye t-shirt. He wasn't as fast as Calypso or even Kara, but he was fast enough to give me pause. "I don't know who y'all are or how you got in here," he said, "but if you're looking for a safe place to hide from the dead outside, well... you'd be better off facing the mob."

"We're just passing through," I said. "And not looking for any trouble."

"Ah, but trouble already found you," the vamp replied.

The rabbi tossed something at the vamp, almost casually, and he snatched it out of the air. It was a tiny vial filled with a greyish-brown powder.

The vamp looked at it and grinned. "Was that supposed to be a distraction or something?"

Rabbi Borovitz frowned. "More like an intelligence test, you shmendrik. *Shabar!*" he said with authority in his voice. The glass vial shattered, and the powder inside filled the air. The vampire began to bat at the dust rapidly with both hands, which only agitated the air and made it worse. Soon his every exposed surface was bubbling and smoking, wherever the dust touched. The vamp shrieked in rage and pain.

"Now would be the time to act, hunter," the old man said with a hint of impatience in his voice. That shocked me into action, and I stepped forward and cut the vamp's head off.

"Silver powder?" I asked.

"Chlorargyrite, to be precise. We were fortunate he was a young one. He has probably never felt the bite of silver before, nor met a human willing to resist him. And he was too dumb to run away."

"Lucky us," I mumbled. "You got any more of that stuff?"

"Unfortunately, that was my last phial."

"Well, hell. Alright then, let's hope we don't run into another one." I dragged the body into a nearby metal cabinet. I stuffed it inside and tossed the head in before I shut the door. "Let's go get that plutonium."

Despite being spread out over several acres, all the buildings on the plant campus were connected by long, enclosed hallways. The benefit to this for us was that those structures blocked off certain areas of the facility from the dead. They might have had the outer cordon surrounded, but there were no dead inside the courtyards between buildings.

That was fortunate, because I didn't want to take the risk of moving from building to building down those hallways. All we needed was to tip our hand by running into another vamp on patrol. For that reason, we opted to sneak to our intended destination by traveling outside the buildings, using safety berms and drainage ditches to hide our passage. The berms had been built to block radiation between one building and another, and the rubber-lined drainage ditches were likely created in case they needed to flush radioactive material from one of the labs.

I wondered how much radioactive material had leached out of the soil over the years, and whether we were unknowingly being fried from the inside out. If we pulled this off and I ended up dying from cancer, I was going to be pissed.

After several tense minutes of sneaking around, we made it to the entrance of one of the underground plutonium storage bunkers. Unfortunately, the vamps were already there, and hard at work trying to get inside. Three pale-skinned figures were working with a cutting torch, diesel generator, and grinder, trying their damnedest to remove the thick steel door to the bunker.

We hid around a corner and observed them for a moment. Between the torch, grinder, and generator, there was no way they were going to hear us. Yet they were smart enough to have the third vamp standing watch—a short stout guy in a dirty jean jacket, sporting a greasy Kenny Powers beard and mullet.

Fortunately, the sentry was currently engrossed in a trashy romance novel, instead of paying attention to his environment. Using hand signals, I indicated that I'd take the guard out, and Josef would take out the others.

There was nowhere to hide and no cover I might use to sneak up on him, so I decided to take the direct approach. I took off my gun belt, scabbard, and ruck sack, and held my sword by the handle near the guard, tip-up and hidden behind my back. I angled it so the last few inches of the blade were concealed behind my head, and casually walked around the corner and toward the sentry with both hands behind my back, as if I were another vampire here to check up on their progress.

The only thing that might give me away was if he sensed I was human, so I tried to move as smoothly and gracefully as possible. I was gambling that he wouldn't be able to hear my heartbeat over the noise. I knew I couldn't hear a damned thing other than the ruckus they were making, and I hoped he couldn't either.

Kenny Powers spotted me immediately, dismissing me with a glance and going right back to reading his novel. But as I got closer, he sensed that something wasn't quite right, and he looked up from his book to examine me more closely.

I smiled. "How's the work coming along?" I asked with casual indifference. I realized my mistake when his eyes widened slightly. *Damn it, Scratch, you don't have the right teeth to be a vamp.* I shrugged. "Mom always said that every time I opened my mouth, it got me in trouble."

The vamp dropped his novel just as I swung the sword up one-handed, slicing the book in two down the spine and opening the vamp up from stem to stern... or sternum, as it were.

He grabbed at his intestines as they spilled out onto the floor, fumbling with the slick, snaky organs that dripped with his dark, almost black blood. I continued the arc of the sword straight overhead, then swung it around in a two-handed cut that took his noggin clean off his shoulders.

JOSEF WAS ALREADY COMING around the corner, but the smell of the sentry's spilled guts must have alerted one of the other vamps. She stopped grinding on the door and flipped up her welder's mask, revealing a thin Anglo face with pockmarks and an overbite that put her upper fangs on full display. Despite her bad complexion, she was attractive in a way that only a vamp or runway model could pull off, somewhat reminiscent of a Cara Delevingne or a young Jessica Lange.

Damn it, I thought. *She couldn't have been older than seventeen when they turned her.*

But innocence had long been lost on that one. She saw Josef and me at the same time, responding with a scowling hiss just as the golem crashed into her and the other vamp. Josef managed to grab the welder by the neck, snapping his neck and rendering him of no consequence instantly.

Unfortunately, overbite girl was quicker and smarter. She quickly recovered from the collision, bouncing into the vault door and launching off it parkour-style. The vamp then proceeded to run sideways along the wall, coming at me with a speed no human could match. Her eyes were murderous, and a wicked yet gleeful smile graced that pretty, pockmarked face.

No doubt about it, she meant to be my death. But I was ready for her, and while she might have been gnawing on any normal human before they could react, I was no normal human. Unable to step out of the way in time, I leaned back like I was playing limbo and raised my blade, severing one of her hands as she passed. The vamp shrieked as she landed in the hall beyond, clutching her stump to her chest.

I saw this all happen in the span of a split-second as I fell to the floor. Josef was already running past me at the little vampire girl, but she was no fool. She hissed one last time and headed down the hall at speed, thankfully ignoring the rabbi as she made her escape.

"Well, shit," I said as I rolled over and stood up.

"Indeed," the rabbi replied. "More of them will be here soon. Josef, if you would be so kind?"

The old man pointed at the thick vault door at the end of the short hall. The golem complied, grabbing it by the handle and a hole that had been made by the cutting torch just moments before. He braced one leg against the wall and strained with all his prodigious strength, yanking on the door with sinew-popping force until the concrete wall around the frame began to crack. Within moments, both the vault door and frame broke away from the wall in a cloud of dust, and Josef let the entire mechanism fall to the floor with a resounding crash.

"I guess that's one way to do it." I looked down and noticed that Kenny Powers' snakeskin boots were sticking out from under the vault door, like the Wicked Witch of the East. "Ding dong, mother—"

The rabbi cut me off. "Yes, yes, we have triumphed over evil, hooray and all that. Now, let us get what we came for before the waif's companions come to finish what she couldn't, *ja*?"

"Fair enough, Rabbi, fair enough."

We entered the storage facility, heading down a short concrete tunnel into a room that was lined with black metal barrels marked "PLANT USE ONLY" in yellow stenciled lettering.

"Huh," I remarked. "I thought the storage containers would be more high-tech."

"What, you expected a yellow metal suitcase with radioactive symbols all over it? This isn't a Michael J. Fox movie, *jaeger*." The rabbi walked up to one of the barrels, rapping it with his knuckles. "This one, Josef—and another, just in case."

I chuckled. "Look at you, old man, with the pop culture references."

He scowled, but his eyes twinkled. "I watched television too, back before all this *scheisse* began."

The golem tucked a barrel under each arm and we headed out of the building, moving as stealthily as we could as we made our way back to the assembly facility. When we arrived, it looked as though we were alone.

"Psst... over here!" I turned to see Kara sticking her head out from behind a large metal door, similar to the one Josef had torn from the wall of the storage bunker. "Bring those barrels in here, then you need to get lost. There's no telling how much radiation is leaking from the plutonium pits inside these containment barrels."

I covered my man parts with my hands. "Great, now you tell me."

Kara rolled her eyes. "I think you'll be fine for the moment, but you probably don't want to be around when I crack them open. Speaking of which, look what I found." She gestured at a large red conical object that was standing nose-down in a made-to-fit rack nearby.

"The warhead, I presume?" She nodded. "So, I take it the rest of the Dallas coven is here?"

She flashed a grim smile. "They must have left a skeleton crew back in Dallas, because there are at least a dozen ancient vamps here. Hell, there's so many younger vamps running around, no one questioned my presence while I was poking about. I grabbed this warhead right in front of a work crew, and no one even gave me a second look."

The rabbi cleared his throat. "About that—we came across a few vampires, and one escaped."

I shrugged sheepishly. "She was too quick for me—for us—to catch. Sorry, but they're probably searching the plant as we speak. How long do you think it'll take you to get this thing armed and get a timer rigged?"

Kara frowned. "I can probably do it in under thirty minutes, working at vampire speed. But, you'll have to keep them away from me while I work."

I looked at the rabbi, and he at me. "We can do that," I said. "But what's the plan after you arm it?"

Kara's eyes went flat and cold. "I'm going to set the warhead to detonate in an hour, and we don't want to be anywhere near here when that happens. It's going to leave a smoldering wasteland a half-mile wide where this plant used to be, incinerating everything biological within that radius."

The rabbi shook his head. "That doesn't seem like a very big window in which to make our escape."

"It's not, but if we hurry we could easily be twenty miles away when it blows. So long as no one finds it before then, that is. I figure if I hide it on top of one of these buildings, they'll never realize it's there until it's too late. I'm also hoping that the increase in elevation will slightly reduce the amount of fallout created by the blast. An air burst would be better, but it's the best I can manage without being able to drop the warhead from high altitude."

"It's a risky plan, but I think that it's our best shot," I said as I looked at my battered military watch. "We'll keep them away from you while you work. When you're done, meet us at our original entry point at the front of the plant."

I turned to go and she stopped me, grabbing me by the shirt. Her eyes spoke volumes as she looked up at me. "Be safe, Scratch. Don't make me come rescue you, alright?"

I kissed her lightly on the lips. "We're just going to play a little game of misdirection, is all. Trust me, I'll be fine."

As soon as we were out of Kara's listening range, I turned to the rabbi. "I am not going to be fine, because there's no way in hell those vamps aren't going to find us."

He nodded. "I agree. What do you intend to do?"

"First, I'm going to create a distraction that'll draw most of the deaders away from the south side of the plant. You think you can get past the stragglers if I do?"

"Ja, Josef will get us safely past them. You wish for me to warn the others?"

I nodded. "The wind is blowing to the southwest, and based on what Kara has told me, it's going to drop fallout a hundred fifty miles or more along Highway 287. So, don't head back the way we came in—instead, take them east of here, then south, as far away as possible. If you have to, lie to them and tell them we have a vehicle, or that Kara is carrying me at vampire speed... hell, I don't care what you tell them. Just make sure you're not within twenty miles of the plant when that warhead goes off."

"I will comply with your wishes. But, Scratch, I must know

—do you intend to make this a one-way mission?"

I paused for a moment before deciding it wouldn't do to lie to the old man. He didn't deserve it, and I suspected he could smell a lie from a mile off anyway.

I smiled, but my eyes were hard. "Rabbi, I intend to give everyone in Texas a fighting chance by making sure those bastards are standing at ground zero when that warhead goes off. If that means I'm there too, so be it."

The rabbi looked at me with sympathetic eyes, and he sighed. "I respect your bravery. There is no time to talk you out of this, so I will simply wish you good luck. And should the worst happen, I will let the others know of your sacrifice."

He extended his hand, and I shook it. "Good luck to you as well, Rabbi. And wait for my signal before you beat feet out of here. You'll know it when you hear it."

He nodded and motioned to Josef, and the golem lifted the rabbi on his shoulders. "Farewell, *jaeger*, and good hunting."

I watched them head away from me down the hall, to ensure they weren't followed. Once they were out of sight, I gathered the materials I needed before exiting the building into one of the inner courtyards. From there, I snuck as far north as I could go, away from the southern side where Rabbi Borovitz and Josef would be making their exit.

No vamps patrolled these inner areas of the plant; whether it was out of laziness, arrogance, or incompetence, I couldn't say. What I did know was that as soon as my distraction went off, they'd come swarming along with the zombie horde. Which meant I needed to be far away when that happened, hopefully at the rally point meeting up with Kara.

Putting all thoughts of failure out of my mind, I dumped the crap I was carrying on the ground and got to work. First, I cleared a space in the dirt, where I placed a scrap piece of metal ductwork that was about two feet in diameter. I poked a shitload of holes in the sides with my knife, then dropped a hundred or so rifle rounds in a neat pile in the center.

I examined my work thus far, wondering how much heat it would take to set the rounds off. *I'd better make it burn hot, just to be safe.*

I crumpled a bunch of discarded reports and inventory checklists I'd found and piled those in the center of the circle. I cracked another round open and sprinkled the gunpowder on top of that, then piled dried brush, grass, and half of an old wooden table I'd smashed apart on top of it all.

I cracked one more round open, sprinkling the gunpowder on a piece of paper that was sticking out of the pile. Finally, I pulled out a disposable lighter and lit it all on fire. The gunpowder went up quickly, setting the paper and kindling alight as it did so. Soon, I had a righteous blaze going inside the little fire pit. I carefully stacked a few more pieces of wood atop the fire, then hauled ass to go find Kara.

I was crossing the courtyard on my way back to meet Kara when I saw them. I'd forgotten that vamps had a keen sense of smell, almost as keen as 'thropes. When the gunpowder had lit, the scent must've caught the attention of one of the patrols, because now there were a half-dozen vamps standing on top of the nearby buildings staring down at me.

They were all model-thin and stunningly beautiful, unlike Kenny Powers and his friends. I noticed the young female vamp who had escaped standing behind them, her head lowered as she clutched her stump to her chest.

"What have we here?" a tall, attractive male vamp said. "A stray hunter, come to kill my brood? Or perhaps a foolish wanderer who decided to take shelter within these walls. One wonders how he got past the millions of zombies and ghouls outside."

"He's the one who cut my arm off, and killed Samuel and Victor," Stump-Girl screeched. "I want him dead! Let me kill him, master, please?"

Master, eh? I should be so lucky. I centered my attention on the vampire she was addressing. He was maybe six-two, with black wavy hair, flawless Mediterranean skin, exotic grey eyes, high cheekbones, and the build of an Olympic swimmer. He wore a dark tailored suit, of a brand that I couldn't recognize except to know that it had cost a lot in the pre-war era. Under the jacket he wore a white dress shirt, left unbuttoned halfway down his chest. Expensive black dress shoes and a gentleman's cane topped off the ensemble; there was a small button where the cane's handle met the shaft.

Sword cane, I noted. *Man, what a walking cliché.*

The vampire popped his cuffs and spun his cane with a casual grace, like Fred Astaire in *Silk Stockings*. My mom had used to love all those old movies, and I'd watched them with her to pass the time when she was at the ranch. The memory made me think of the vamp who'd turned my dad, all those years ago. Dad's descent into blood-frenzied madness had destroyed Mom's spirit, and she'd ended her own life the day after she'd put him out of his suffering. I'd laid them both to rest at the ranch, side-by-side, just like they would have wanted.

Those memories steeled my resolve, reminding me of how we'd gotten to this point in human history—scattered, hunted, and all but extinct as a species. An ember sparked inside my chest, an old hatred that I'd kept smoldering within since my parents had passed and everything had gone to hell in a handbasket.

And the assholes standing right in front of me were ultimately to blame.

Yeah, I'm going to see that you all burn to ash and dust.

The speaker gestured slightly at Stump-Girl, without glancing in her direction. "Hush, child. You don't decide who lives or dies, who feeds or starves, or who we spare or sacrifice."

The girl dropped to her knees and bowed low to the ground. "I beg your forgiveness, master." Her voice shook as she spoke.

I decided to up the ante. It was apparent this vamp wasn't accustomed to anyone talking back to him, so I figured I'd try to get his hackles up while my distraction was cooking. I drew my katana in one hand and pointed it at him.

"So, you're the master of the Dallas coven?"

One of the vamps in the peanut gallery hissed. These pretty vamps seemed to hiss a lot, I'd noticed. Again, the master vamp quieted the outburst with a gesture, and the vamp who'd vocalized her displeasure hung her head.

Damn, but how they all fear this guy. He has to be their head honcho.

"I am," the master vamp replied. "My name is Marduk, and you'd do well to fear it." He pronounced his name like "Mah-ROO-duke," trilling the "r" in the second syllable.

I cupped my hand to my left ear, as if I was trying to listen more closely. "I'm sorry... Marmaduke? Like the dog in the comics?"

He smirked, and his voice held genuine amusement as he replied. "No, you impetuous mortal. Like the Babylonian god."

"Ah, I see." I nodded sagely as I drew a line in the dirt with the tip of my sword. "Well, *Marduk*, I'm the guy who took out Piotr and Calypso. I take it they were your star students or some such, the way they strutted and crowed. Yet in the end they died, just like all the other vamps I've killed. I eighty-sixed the other two losers that crack whore of a bloodsucker was with earlier, and I'll go down fighting before I let you assholes feed on me. So, draw that toothpick you carry inside that cane, and let's see what you're made of."

He cocked his head to one side, pursing his lips as he nodded. "I applaud your composure in the face of certain death, human. And as you've made it this far, I can see how you might have caught my children unawares."

The ancient vamp drew his sword in one fluid motion, tossing the cane shaft that served as a scabbard to a nearby vamp, who caught it with ease. "But no matter—I'll avenge their deaths by first teaching you how wrong you are to challenge me. And when your spirit is broken and you're bleeding from a thousand wounds, I'll allow the remainder of my children to fall on you and feed until you're nothing but an empty husk."

I spun my sword in circles to loosen up my wrist. "Well then, you're a daisy if you do. *En garde*, bloodsucker."

THE MASTER VAMPIRE closed the gap between us in the blink of an eye, too fast for me to see. Instantly, the battle was on. He fought with a fencer's skill, all panache and form, attacking from a dozen different angles. It soon became obvious that he was playing with me, as I was able to block most of his initial thrusts and cuts, and backpedal away to avoid the rest.

If he was coming at me for real, I'd already be dead.

A curious tilt of his head and the slight twitch of an eyebrow told me I'd surprised him by fending off his attacks, half-hearted or not.

"Your skills are crude, but I see you do have some training," he said. "There are so few warriors left in this world, so few humans who are worthy of the gift." He shook his head slightly, and his eyes grew almost sad. "It will be a shame to have to kill you. A warrior such as you could have served me well."

"I'd die first," I growled.

"As you wish," he replied. Marduk whirred past me, and suddenly I was bleeding from a shallow cut across my cheek.

"Oh come on, not the face," I quipped. "I was just getting used to the scars on the other side."

He looked at me with the curious detachment of a child preparing the pull the legs off a bug, just to see what would happen. "Fearlessness in the face of death is indeed a commendable trait. However, you'll not be in good humor for long, I'm afraid. Again, such a shame to have to kill you."

He flitted around and cut me dozens of times, too fast to see, much less block. Each cut was scalpel-clean and just deep enough for blood to flow freely, without causing a debilitating injury. It was clear that he intended to do exactly as he said, to bleed me from a thousand cuts and break my spirit. My clothes soon dripped with blood, and I began to feel the first signs of shock.

I feigned being weaker than I was, hoping for an overconfidence that I might capitalize on. I had to get at least one good stroke in, after all. Marduk was within attacking range and his guard was down, so I stepped forward and swung at him with everything I had. Despite the blood loss, it was still probably the quickest I'd ever moved in my life.

The master vampire casually leaned away from my cut, allowing it to pass him harmlessly. Determined to keep him occupied as long as possible, I unleashed a flurry of cuts, thrusts, and slashes, attacking with combinations that would have felled any human and most supernatural creatures. Yet he moved only slightly each time, just enough to make my attacks miss by mere centimeters.

And while adrenaline fueled my efforts, all that movement caused my wounds to bleed even more freely. My arms grew heavy and my legs numb; I began to grow lightheaded and dizzy, and my heart beat faster due to blood loss. I staggered forward and swung at him one last time with the same result as before. I stumbled to my knees as his final, desultory evasion caused me to lose my balance.

Come on, Scratch, don't die just yet. Gotta give the rabbi a fighting chance to get back and warn the kids and Sledge, and give Kara time to set up that bomb. Just a few more seconds —there!

Rifle ammunition cooked off in the distance, and even with the rumble of millions of feet outside the plant and the moans of all those walking dead, the sound split the night like thunder. *Pop. Pop-pop. Pop-pop-pop!* As the rounds went off, the moans of the dead grew louder and louder, and the ground began to rumble as thousands of shamblers drew toward the disturbance.

The walls of the plant began to groan against the force of thousands of agitated dead who were desperately trying to find the source of that noise.

Moments before, all eyes had been on me, the blood bag the coven was about to turn into a snackpack. Now, some of the vamps were distracted by the gunfire, while others were looking nervously at the throng of dead outside the plant. Never one to miss an opportunity to slay the undead, I drew my sidearm and shot two of the closest vamps in the head, just before I collapsed completely.

"Man, that felt good," I rasped.

Marduk's eyes snapped to the two vampires I'd killed, then to me. "Enough!" he shouted, moving forward in a blur and knocking my weapons from my hands.

I cackled drunkenly, dizzy with blood loss. "That's two more down, Marduk. Seems like you're in desperate need of a recruitment drive. You sure you want to feed me to your kids?"

His lips curled into a snarl. "I grow tired of your insolence." He pointed at Stump-Girl. "You, go see if you can put a stop to that gunfire." The girl nodded and sped away into the night.

Marduk gestured to the rest of the coven. "The rest of you may feed."

More than a half-dozen vampires fell on me like crows on ripe corn. The lot of them began licking and sucking at my

222 / M.D. MASSEY

wounds, tearing through my clothing to get at what remained of my warm, fresh blood.

Seconds later, the lot of them began gagging and coughing. They retched and convulsed as their mouths and tongues turned black, smoldering and bubbling as if they'd ingested acid rather than heme and plasma.

As the vampires fell away from me, I wheezed out a weak but satisfying laugh.

"Oh yeah, I forgot to mention. My blood is poison to the undead."

The master vampire looked around at the scene before him in utter disbelief. "What magic is this? Did you ingest silver, or did the druid cast some spell or curse on your lifeblood?"

With no small amount of effort, I lifted my head so I could look him in the eye. "See here, Marmaduke. I don't know any druids, and I sure as hell didn't let anyone cast any hoodoo on me. This is one-hundred percent modern science, pure and simple." I laughed again and dropped my head back to the ground, keeping my eyes on him so I could see his reaction. "Oh, this is rich."

Marduk looked around at his dying coven with frantic desperation in his eyes. "Tell me how to reverse it. Tell me how to save my offspring!"

I reached up and wiped a drop of blood from my eye. "You're talking to the wrong individual there, Count Chocula. I don't know a damned thing about how this stuff all works. And the only person who does is hundreds of miles away. Good luck finding them before your kiddos all croak."

Marduk hung his head. The rounds had stopped going off, but the dead were beginning to crawl over the walls to get inside the courtyard. When they finished their rampage, the plant would be in shambles, that much was clear. And Marduk might have some of the materials he needed to bring more of his kind over from across the Veil—but who would carry his plan out, now that nearly his entire coven was dying or dead?

Sure, he might have had additional vamps back in Dallas, and he could make more from whatever humans he kept as cattle. But I had a feeling all his remaining heavy hitters were now choking on my blood.

Too bad I didn't manage to trick him into feeding on me as well, I thought.

Yet none of that would matter shortly. If everything had gone to plan, the rabbi would be heading south with the kids and Sledge, and Kara would have already set the warhead to go off. I might have been dying, but Marduk and the entire horde of deaders would be one giant ash heap within minutes.

Marduk raised his head again, and he glowered at me murderously as he took a step toward me. "You will pay for your treachery, and it will be no easy death."

I had no illusions about what would happen next. This guy was going to rip me limb from limb in the most literal manner possible, and there was absolutely nothing I could do about it. *Kara, I hope you got away safe.*

Then he was standing over me, transformed into something that was a bit of a cross between a higher vamp and a nosferatu. His brow and cheekbones protruded, his jaw was thicker, and his skin had taken on an ashen color. I noted also that his fingers were tipped in claws now, and his teeth had elongated. His eyes were dark red orbs, the color of old blood—all except for those silver irises and the black pupils within.

Truth was, I was ready to go. I looked up at him and shrugged. "Well, I suppose there are worse ways to die. Fire always scared the shit out of me, and drowning. Being dropped

224 / M.D. MASSEY

into a vat of acid, now there's a nasty way to die. Nah, believe me, you won't get the satisfaction of hearing me scream."

"Then know this: I will hunt down every last person you care for, everyone you love. The woman Piotr turned. The child. The alpha's son. The scientist. All the people you've helped during your short, miserable existence. They will all be destroyed, and your legacy will mean nothing."

He meant it, too. I sighed. "Let me get this straight... you intend to kill me, and *then* go after everyone I love? What will it matter then? Shit, I'll be dead and gone, oblivious to whatever the hell you decide to do. Seems like what you really want to do is keep me alive, so I can live to see all that come to pass." I lifted my hands up in supplication. "But hey, you're the immortal vampire master. Don't let me tell you how to do your job."

He shook his head. "I've been on this earth since the dawn of civilization, hunter. Do you think I don't see through your feeble attempts to manipulate me into sparing you? No, it's time for you to die, and I'll take great comfort in knowing that your final thoughts will be of pain, mingled with regret over how you've damned those you love."

He knelt beside me and grabbed my wrist. I struggled against his grip, but I might as well have been arm wrestling with Godzilla. With his other hand, he grasped my pinky finger firmly and plucked it from the socket like he was plucking a petal from a flower.

I stifled my scream. Despite being dizzy with blood loss, it hurt like hell to lose that finger. "Ah, damn you, you motherfucker!" I growled.

His weird silver and crimson eyes lit up at my response, and I was pretty sure he was sporting a woody. "Now, that's the spirit." He plucked the next finger off.

"Grrrr... fuck!" I couldn't help it. I screamed like a banshee.

Marduk purred like a werecat experiencing her first orgasm.

"Ah, that is such a delightful sound. Tell me, hunter, do you know how long a person can live, after their limbs have been torn off? I do. With a few carefully-placed tourniquets, it's possible to keep a human alive for some time after being dismembered. But in your condition, well... let's just see how long I can keep you from dying, hmm?"

I looked him in the eye and swung at him with my other hand. He blocked the punch nonchalantly with his free hand, then grabbed my middle finger. At that moment, two things happened.

First, Marduk's eyes grew wide, and he blurred away from me.

Second, I heard the report of a large-caliber rifle just as droplets of dark vampire blood and gibbets of cold flesh peppered my face and body.

Marduk stood about ten feet away, with a huge gaping hole in the left side of his chest. And fifty feet away on a nearby roof, Kara was frantically working the bolt on her fifty-caliber Barrett sniper rifle.

Must have been going for the heart. Shit. The only thing I could figure was that Marduk had heard the snap of the trigger breaking, just before the firing pin dropped and the primer ignited. He'd moved fast enough so that she had missed his heart. But I thought that surely, despite being an ancient vampire, a fifty-caliber silver round to the chest would have taken him out.

Apparently, I was wrong.

Marduk looked up at Kara with rage. "You insignificant speck of shit—how dare you!" he bellowed, despite the fact that he was missing most of his right lung. I didn't get how that worked, until I saw that his wound was already closing up. I didn't think a vamp could heal like that without ingesting fresh blood—but again, I was wrong. This Marduk fellow seemed to be breaking all the rules.

In the blink of an eye, he had Kara by the neck, her legs dangling off the roof of the building. He was going to snap her spine, I was certain of it. I sat up slowly, looking around for a weapon—my sword, a rifle, something.

Then I heard Tony's voice echoing in my head. *If you gotta go out in a blaze of glory, well—injecting that shit will make it happen.* I began patting my pockets, hoping against hope that the damned autoinjector hadn't been smashed when the vamps were feeding on me. Finally, my nearly numb fingers landed on a hard, cylindrical object in my pants pocket.

I looked up, and Kara's face was turning purple as Marduk slowly squeezed the life out of her. I popped the safety cap off the injector, then slammed it into my chest over my heart, just to make sure it injected where there was enough circulation to matter. For a moment, nothing happened.

Then...

Thud-thud. Thud-THUD. THUD-THUD. My heart began beating like the intro to Van Halen's "Hot For Teacher" as feeling and strength flowed back into my limbs. My dizziness subsided, and any anxiety and pain I had felt faded away, to be replaced with a fire in my belly and laser focus on the task at hand.

I saw my sword in the grass, just yards away. I *moved*, and suddenly it was in my hand. I looked up, in time to see the light dying in Kara's eyes.

"No!" I leapt from where I stood, almost flying through the air at them. Marduk wasn't even paying attention to me, so focused was he on killing Kara. She was likely the only vampire who'd defied him in centuries, and it was to my momentary advantage that his rage had clouded his senses.

As I landed on the roof, I severed Marduk's arm at the elbow, shouldering him away in the same motion. I caught Kara with my damaged arm and hand as she fell, and pried the ancient vampire's dismembered hand away from her throat.

Kara wasn't moving. *How can you tell if a vampire is dead, or if they've merely fainted?* I wondered.

I shook her, hoping to get some response. "Kara, wake up, baby. Oh, please don't die on me—not like this."

Nothing.

I turned to find Marduk standing in the courtyard looking up at me, holding his sword cane in his remaining hand. The wound in his chest had closed, and the skin on his right arm had already grown over his stump.

His eyes narrowed as he regarded me, and a silent, barely controlled rage was etched on his face. "If you hadn't challenged me earlier, I'd have killed you while you lingered over your lover's corpse. But needs be that some honor is left in this world, however meaningless. Come, hunter. Face your end with a dignity deserving of a warrior."

I stood and hissed my reply. "I wonder, vampire—how long can one of your kind live after being dismembered?"

Then I launched myself off the roof at him, with a speed that managed to surprise even the vampire. Our blades clanged together once, twice, three times in an instant. He was still faster than me, but I had something on my side that he didn't. I was used to fighting things that were stronger, faster, and hardier than me. Marduk, on the other hand, wasn't accustomed to being challenged at all.

I sprung away from him while avoiding a nasty backhanded slash that would've taken my head off. After that clash, I knew I couldn't beat him cleanly, even with the drug cocktail Tony had given me. But I wasn't thinking about winning.

I was only thinking about not losing.

Marduk gave me a knowing grin. I noticed that while his stance was relaxed, his sword wasn't, as the tip was pointed right at me. "You fight well, hunter, and whatever power you've drawn on to bring you back from the brink of death is impressive. But you are still dying, and despite this rally you will lose."

"Shut up and fight," I whispered, springing at him with a flurry of cuts that he danced away from, parrying each one with relative ease. *C'mon, you overconfident prick—make your move.* I saw something in his eyes, a tell I'd noticed earlier. The asshole always looked where he was going to thrust.

As he moved, so did I. Not away from him, but at him. I took the sword thrust square in the ribs, pulling him into me so I could lay my blade against his throat. I extended my arm in a full draw cut, pressing hard as twenty-four inches of razor-sharp *tamahagane* steel sliced through his ancient flesh like a hot knife through butter.

I smiled grimly at him as his eyes grew wide. The rest of his body froze, bereft of any signal from his brain that might tell it to rip his sword out of my chest to finish me. His lips and jaw worked, but no sound came forth, and his head slowly slid from his shoulders, tumbling away into the grass next to us.

I pushed the vampire's headless corpse away from me, sliding myself off his blade as his body fell. Then I flipped my own blade around and took a single step, falling to my knees with a downward thrust. My blade skewered the vamp's head like an olive on a toothpick, pinning it to the ground through one eye and out the back of his skull.

Then, everything went black.

DARKNESS. *Motion. Voices.* I was in a moving vehicle. Fragments of conversation came to me as I faded in and out.

"...have to do it, Sledge..."

"...his only chance..."

"...might not even work..."

"...half-dead already..."

"...no other choice..."

"Fine, but it's not on me if it doesn't take. I've never seen someone survive the change when they were this close to death. You sure about this?"

I felt someone caress my face, as Kara's voice came loud and clear from nearby. "Do it."

Pain overtook me, and I faded from consciousness.

I had no idea how long I was out, but when I woke I was in my bed back at the Facility. Kara was sitting in a chair next to me, while Gabby was pacing at the foot of the bed.

"You can stop walking a hole in the floor, kid. I'm awake."

I was sitting up, slowly, when a ninety-pound missile practically tackled me. The kid buried her head in my chest and wrapped me in a bear hug. I hugged her back, patting her back with one arm while noting the two pink-skinned nubs where my fingers had once been.

The kid broke away, shoving me in the chest with both hands. "What the hell is wrong with you?" she cried. "You had us worried sick!" Tears were streaming down her face.

"Hey, it's alright. I'm alive, I think." I looked around at the I.V. in my arm, and examined the dozens of fresh scars all over my body. "Not going to be winning any beauty contests, though." I looked at Kara. "Whose idea was it to turn me?"

She tilted her head, her eyes glassy. I think if a vampire could cry, she'd have been shedding tears. "It was a group decision. Sledge did the honors. Bobby didn't know if he could do it, at his age. Plus, he'd never turned anyone before, but Sledge had." Kara's voice grew soft. "Are you mad?"

I chewed my lip and nodded. "A little. Should've been my choice, but I'm not going to complain about y'all saving my life." I looked around the room, and tuned my hearing to what was going on in the hall. Voices and footsteps came at me from all directions in stereoscopic sound, adding a sense of depth and distance to what I heard.

Kara recognized the shock on my face. "It'll take some getting used to. Give it a few days."

"Uh-huh. Where's Bobby?"

Gabby cleared her throat. "He said he couldn't just sit around waiting for you to wake up... something about too much nervous energy. He's been running patrols almost non-stop for days."

"How long was I out?" I asked.

Kara grunted. "Ten days. We hunkered down for a week in the basement of an abandoned house in Lubbock, making sure the fallout had dispersed before we headed back here. The Doc and I have been taking dosimeter and Geiger readings since we got back, and thankfully everything around here seems all clear."

"Any sign of the vamps since Amarillo?"

Kara shook her head. "None. But we're running short-range and long-range patrols, keeping an eye out just in case."

"What about deaders?"

Gabby smirked. "Aunt Lorena got the pest control system working again. We're officially a dead-free zone."

"Sounds like you have everything in hand." I laid my head back down on the pillow, and closed my eyes. "So, if y'all don't mind, I'm going back to sleep."

Despite having werewolf healing abilities, I spent several more days recuperating. The fingers never did grow back, and my scars never went away. Samson said that the 'thrope vyrus only worked with what you had when you were turned, and that it didn't restore what you'd lost before then. I was just glad that Marduk hadn't had a chance to tear anything important off before Kara had shot him.

In the weeks following our return from Amarillo, talk turned to what we'd do if more vamps showed up, and how we might distribute the vaccine the Doc had cooked up. It wouldn't get rid of the deaders or the vamps, but at least it'd prevent more humans from turning. That was something, at least.

Although we hadn't seen hide or hair of the vamps, I was still the paranoid type. So, I got with Samson and we sent a small recon team up to Dallas to see what was up.

When the scouts returned, they reported that the Dallas coven had fallen into disarray since the events that occurred in

Amarillo. The remaining vamps had sent their own people to find out what had happened to Marduk and the rest of the coven, and once they'd determined he was gone for good, war broke out. All the baby vamps started killing each other, and not one of them had a clue how to make new vampires.

The result was that what remained of the Dallas coven had destroyed itself from the inside out. Only a few vamps were left standing, and they controlled only small pockets of the walled citadel the vamps had constructed after the War and invasion. But they still had all the infrastructure they'd built: electricity derived from solar and wind power, clean water, lots of living space, and walls to keep the whole thing deader-free.

It was too good an opportunity to pass up. We fell on them like locusts during the day, killing them all and freeing the thousand or so humans who'd been kept as servants and cattle. Having learned my lesson from Nadine, we vaccinated and exiled any troublemakers who were unwilling to pull their weight or toe the line.

As for the rest? We armed and trained them, of course.

Within months, we had the largest militia in Texas, controlling what had become the safest and most secure area in the state. Once our reputation spread, it was only a matter of time before more survivors started showing up. Some came due to rumors of a vaccine, while others came looking for the sort of safe haven they'd never known.

Within time, rumors spread among the population about a serum that gave you powers, and about humans who'd become 'thropes. People started volunteering for one or both, so they could join the fight.

We needed a plan. Samson, Anna, Colin, Kara, the Doc, and I came up with one.

The Pack agreed to work with the humans to rebuild civilization, starting with Dallas first. The ultimate goal was to get the vaccine to every major remaining outpost in the state, and to organize more militia to eradicate the dead and keep the vamps at bay.

The only thing was, I knew it wouldn't be enough.

So, I came up with the idea of creating elite units that were patterned after special forces A Teams, with a 'thrope as the heavy hitter, four juiced hunters serving in different tactical roles, and a human magic user trained by Colin to work the hoodoo. The idea was that these teams would be sent out to distribute the vaccine, establish outposts, and train insurgent militia units. And, they'd be able to troubleshoot problem areas that contained pockets of resistance, taking out vamps, revenants, and the like that the human militia couldn't handle.

Everyone agreed that it was a good plan, and we started implementing it immediately. Inside of a year we controlled everything north of Dallas to Wichita Falls and Texarkana, and south to Laredo and Corpus Christi. Houston was a wasteland of dead, so we left it alone, relying on the refineries along the Gulf Coast further south for petroleum processing. We trained medical personnel, started clinics in every outpost, and encouraged people to settle in reclaimed areas.

All told, it was a massive success. But people and vamps didn't mix, and I knew it was only a matter of time before Kara got found out. There was just too much negative sentiment against her kind for her to ever be able to coexist with humans.

Besides, the clamor of the city and so-called civilization just wasn't for me, and the way things were running I'd become a redundancy. Gabby, Bobby, and Colin ran the teams, Samson kept the 'thropes in order, and Anna headed up the human militia. A council led and voted on everything, and we'd even put a Constitution in place, with laws and rules and all the happy horse shit that keeps a society from imploding.

At that point, I knew I'd done my part, and I was satisfied to rest easy in the knowledge that they'd all be just fine without me.

It was time to go home.

Kara and I spent days getting the ranch house back in order. Scavs had been through, but they hadn't stayed since there wasn't much of use to take that I hadn't hidden. My caches remained untouched, which meant we were good on weapons, ammo, and gear. Not that we needed the firepower, but I felt better with a gun on my hip just the same.

We were sitting out on the porch late one evening, enjoying the night air and each other's company, when we heard them coming up the drive. It was a small group, maybe five or six men and women, walking like they were carrying heavy packs and lots of gear. From the sounds of it, they were armed.

"I told you they'd come," Kara said sadly.

I grabbed my rifle and laid it across my lap. I waited until they were within shouting distance before speaking.

"Y'all lost?" I said, loud enough to be heard clearly.

The footsteps stopped. We heard them whispering, so we waited for them to decide who should speak. Moments later, matters were settled and an older woman's voice hollered back from down the hill.

"Not rightly—that is to say, not if this is the Sullivan place."

I looked at Kara, and she raised an eyebrow and shrugged.

"It is," I replied. "Dangerous for you folk to be out at night. What business you got here?"

The old woman paused. "Are you the Sullivan boy? The one who used to hunt these parts, looking out for the settlements?"

I looked at Kara, who replied with another shrug. "I am."

"We got need for a hunter, mister."

"Shoulda sent for the militia, out east. There's an outpost in Fredericksburg, you know."

She laughed, but her tone was devoid of humor. "We did. Said they don't come out to these parts, outta respect. Said you told 'em to steer clear."

Kara chuckled. "Told you that would bite you in the ass."

"That you did," I said softly. "What do you think?"

"Other than being nervous about approaching you, as far as I can tell they're not lying. Heart rates are more or less normal, and I don't smell fear—only a bit of nervousness."

"Damn it," I whispered. "What's your situation, lady?" I shouted.

The woman's voice held a spark of hope that hadn't been there before. "We got a rev' that's been harassing us real bad. Mean one, and crafty. Sent men after it, but they ain't come back. We need help, mister."

"You got kids with you?"

"Couldn't very well leave them back home, could we? They's hidin' down the hill."

Kara laid a hand on my arm. "Scratch, you can't turn them away."

I closed my eyes and sighed. "Fine," I muttered. I stood and raised my voice again. "Y'all fetch those kids and come up to the house. You can get some hot food in you while I grab my gear."

The love of my life leaned over to lay a soft, cold kiss on my cheek. She stood and headed inside. "I'll heat that stew up you made earlier and whip up some fry bread." Kara paused at the doorway, gracing me with a mischievous grin. "But I'm coming with you, once we get them settled."

I returned her smile, my heart swelling. "I wouldn't have it any other way."

This concludes the Scratch Sullivan saga.
Want more paranormal action and mystery? Go to
http://mdmassey.com/books/ to check out my other novels,
including the Colin McCool paranormal suspense series and
novellas.